The Dandelion Garden

The Dandelion Garden

and Other Stories

Budge Wilson

Philomel Books   New York

Library of Congress Cataloging-in-Publication Data
Wilson, Budge.   The dandelion garden/Budge Wilson.   p.   cm.
Summary: A collection of short stories about friendships, family relationships,
and the trials of growing up.
1. Short stories, Canadian.   [1. Short stories.   2. Canada—Fiction.]   I. Title.
PZ7.W69004Dan 1995   [Fic]—dc20   94-26641 CIP AC
ISBN 0-399-22768-7

10 9 8 7 6 5 4 3 2 1

First Impression

This book is for
Donna and Murray Forbes

*The following stories have been previously published
in a somewhat different form:*

"Big Little Jerome" in *Crackers,* 1985; in *Reading and Responding,* 1991.
"The Canoe Trip" in *Islands in the Harbour,* Roseway Publishing, 1990;
in *The Courtship,* House of Anansi Press Limited, 1994.
"The Charmer," "Cordelia Clark," "Dreams," "The Happy Pill," and "Joanna
and the Dark" in *Cordelia Clark,* Stoddart Publishing Co., Limited, 1994.
"Janetta's Confinement" in *The Courtship,* House of Anansi Press Limited, 1994.
"Was It Fun on the Beach Today?" in *The Blue Jean Collection,* Thistledown
Press, 1992; in *Cordelia Clark,* Stoddart Publishing Co. Limited, 1994.

Contents

The Charmer

I am thirty-three years old now, and I no longer wake up each morning with a hard lump of anger pressing against my chest.

It seems I've come full circle. Way back when I was a little girl, I was not angry at all, not ever. Like everyone else, I was too charmed to be irritated. No. But perhaps *charmed* is too mild a term. At that age, I felt something more intense. I was bewitched. My heart lay open and eager. He could take it and me, and do with us what he would. When he beckoned, I followed, at top speed. If he said, "How about you wash my bike for me, Posie, love?" I would be halfway to the kitchen for a bucket and rags before he stopped speaking. When he said, "Go get my baseball, kid," I ran and got it. "Thanks, Posie," he'd say, grabbing the ball and disappearing to the park.

My name is not Posie. It's Winnifred. Winnifred means "friend of peace." Later I would have a grim laugh or two about that. He always called me Posie when he wanted me to do something for him, or when he wished to make it clear to me that I had measured up. It was payment for good behavior, and an insurance policy for future services. Collect his baseball and I will get my reward—his flashing Colgate smile and my pet name.

He was my brother.

His name was Zackary, and he was eleven years older than I was. Wouldn't you know they'd call him Zackary and me Winnifred? Zackary has such an exotic ring to it, and when all his friends took to calling him Zack, it was like he was a movie star or a TV hero or something. It has always seemed to me that the most compellingly male, the most electric movie and rock stars, have short names. I watch a lot of late-night movies on the tube, and I should know. Clark Gable, John Wayne, Kirk Douglas, Steve McQueen. And nearer to the present day, Mick Jagger, John Lennon, Matt Dillon. Take Tyrone Power, now. A lot of women have admired Tyrone Power. But to my way of thinking, he was as flimsy, as pretty, as his name.

But Winnifred. Winnifred is on a par with Edna, Maud, Ernestine—terrible names, all of them. It's true that, for a while, I thought that Winnifred might be special. In Sunday school, we had a hymn that went:

> *Winnie cometh, Winnie cometh,*
> *To make up His jewels . . .*

The hymns were thrown onto a screen, in huge block letters, and at first I was too young to read the words. What delicious prestige to be that Winnie who everyone was singing about! Placed in a hymn and written on the wall for all to see. Chosen to become His jewels—rubies, diamonds, opals. Then, of course, I learned to read, and found out the truth.

> *When He cometh, when He cometh,*
> *To make up His jewels . . .*

And I realized I'd be precious lucky to be even one of those jewels. Besides, I wasn't really Winnie, anyway. I was Winnifred. Don't ask me why, but I just wasn't the kind of kid who ended up with a nickname. So you can imagine the effect that "Posie" had upon my spirit. As early as three years old, I knew that posies were a bouquet of flowers.

◆　　◆　　◆

I was Zackary's willing slave. Slavery, in fact, was in vogue in our house. Mom would make a chocolate layer cake for the church bazaar and leave it on the kitchen table with a sign beside it: FOR CHURCH BAZAAR. DEATH TO ANYONE WHO TOUCHES IT. Chances are she'd arrive home from town, two hours before the bazaar, to find a large piece cut out of the side, crumbs all over the floor, and the sign turned upside down.

Then Zack would come home just as she was tying on her apron to make another cake. Brown from the sun, black curls glistening from the municipal pool, he would enter the kitchen, dancing a little jig on the doormat. His mouth would go all mock-sad and quivering at the corners. "My mother, my queen!" he might say. "How could someone with any taste buds at all ignore the creation of so great a cook? The master chef of the whole of this city!" Then he would give her one of his special bear hugs. Or he might get down on one or even both of his knees. "Forgive me, Duchess," he would say, and then unbutton his shirt, laying bare his marvelous brown chest. "For the knife," he would say. "For death."

Then my mother would laugh, we'd *all* laugh, and Mom would mix up the batter for the new cake, a smile playing upon her lips. "Go ahead!" she'd say, with a fake sigh.

"Have another piece. You certainly are the limit!" My two little sisters and I would stand there grinning, while Zack sat down and ate half the cake. Then the three of us would wash up the old baking dishes and the new baking dishes and his plate and fork and glass. And sweep up his crumbs. Before he left, he would probably bow low once more to Mom, and say, "Thank you, my angel." She'd put her head on one side, with that adoring look of hers, and say, "Be off with you! You're a real devil!"

Which, of course, he was. But anyone who knows anything about devils knows that they're fallen angels, and can often fool you for a very long time. We studied a chunk of *Paradise Lost* in grade twelve. Milton's Satan certainly had a lot more going for him than the angels who hovered over the garden, exuding piety.

Even Dad took a long time to wake up. You wouldn't think a fourteen- or sixteen-year-old boy could hoodwink a father, but he could, he could. Zack lied over trifles, and periodically stole money out of wallets that were left lying around. He started smoking at thirteen, and was into the liquor cabinet by fourteen. At sixteen, he smashed up our car one night after a poker party. Once he dumped Dad's red toolbox, tools and all, in the river, during one of his rages. The toolbox seemed to bother Dad even more than

The Dandelion Garden

the car. But afterwards, Zack would deliver apologies that would have brought tears to a preacher's eyes. That kind of dramatic repentance has a lot more clout than simple everyday good behavior, and he really knew how to pull it off. Zack'd been in Sunday school himself long enough to be able to quote from the Prodigal Son on appropriate occasions, and for the first twenty-two or so times he did it, he really convinced us when he said he was "no longer worthy to be called thy son." The part about making him "one of thy hired servants" always left Mom in tatters. Later on, Dad would just leave the room and go out to his work shed and sit and rock and rock in that old chair of his.

People probably thought we were deficient in brain power to be taken in by such cheap tricks. But just try putting yourself in our shoes. He was the only son, the only brother, the oldest child. He was intelligent and fun, and knew how to coax laughter out of a stone. He was surrounded by a bevy of admirers; everywhere he went, he trailed friends. He was athletic, won races, amassed trophies. He got lead parts in school plays. He won class elections. And he was beautiful. His face was rugged and laughing; his body was muscular and golden, even in January. He moved with the grace of a tiger. He dazzled. He shone.

By the time I was thirteen, Zackary's halo was dimming,

6

but I still adored him. He was twenty-four years old, still living at home, still guzzling chocolate cakes, still borrowing the car. He needed money for his girlfriends and his liquor and his poker, and home was a cheap place to live. Cranky and delightful, moody and captivating, he still played the hero's role in our house.

Then Lizzie got sick. She wasn't just sick. She had leukemia, and every one of us knew she was going to die. She was the youngest, the quiet one, the gentle one. She idolized Zack even more than the rest of us, because she was only seven, too young to see any of his flaws. He was her knight in shining armor, and she was forever looking for him to ride by her hospital room. "Why doesn't Zack come?" she kept asking. Once, just once, he arrived with a comic book for her, and her white little face lit up so brightly that you could almost convince yourself she might get better. He even made her laugh, and all our hearts went out to him in gratitude. But apart from that, he never once visited her during those last awful six weeks in the hospital. He was on drinking rampages day after day, or else he'd sober up enough to spend a week trying to win liquor money at the poker table.

One day Mom had the courage to plead, "Please, Zackary. Go see Lizzie. She keeps asking for you. *Please*."

He sat down and put his head in his hands, saying, "I'm in terrible pain, Mom. I'm so frustrated. I can't help her." To which she replied, stiffly, "You can. You can visit her."

Then he rose from his chair and threw a book on the floor. "Quit nagging!" he snapped at her. "I'm too old for that. I can handle my own life. I don't need you telling me what to do."

Zack lost a job and got another, and then lost that one, too. He was forever taking off in the family car, just as we were needing it to go to the hospital. But Mom forgave him for everything. "He's sensitive," she'd say. "He's taking it hard, and he can't face what's ahead for us. This is his way of coping. He's probably suffering more than the rest of us." Suffering, my foot, I thought.

That last day, the day that Lizzie died, we were all at the hospital to watch it happen—all, of course, except Zackary. Then the nurse came in and said that no, she was not asleep, she was gone.

There she was, our Lizzie, tubes coming out of her all over, machines ticking away, and nothing left of her at all. I tasted the words, "Gone. Dead," and they had no meaning at all for me. The closest I could come to a definition was "Not there anymore," but this was too large a concept for me to absorb. I could understand only the rage and the grief.

When we all walked out into the corridor, there he was. Zackary. Sobered up, dressed in the outfit Lizzie loved best: the tight jeans and the Mickey Mouse shirt. He stood there grinning, his arms overflowing with gifts—a hot-pink teddy bear, a bundle of comics, a Barbie doll in a bride's dress, a bouquet of five orchids. *Hail, the conquering hero comes.* Orchids, I thought. *Orchids.* I fled to the hospital washroom and was sick into the basin.

Four days later, he came home. He'd been heaven-knows-where in the meantime. He had on a clean white shirt, open at the neck, and his jeans. It was summer, and his skin was shining, gleaming, tanned, so that you knew he'd been at the beach a lot—down the South Shore, maybe. He'd never looked more handsome. Scudding across my mind came the thought: If you can't find a job, Zack, try Sears catalogue, Men's Clothing division. You're a photographer's dream.

He sat down, head in his hands, of course. Don't move, I silently begged my mother. *Don't move.* But she went over and sat down beside him, placing her hand on his back. Then the words came, but no tears. "I'm sorry. I'm sorry," and variations on the theme. Start the Prodigal Son bit, I thought, and I'll kill you. But he did. ". . . no longer worthy to be called thy son," he finished, his voice suitably uneven. "Make me as one of thy hired servants." My mother was kissing his hand and crying. I had a terrible desire to spit. Thirteen years old and a girl, and it was all I could do to keep from standing up and spitting on the carpet beside his feet. My father did stand up.

"I agree one hundred percent," he said, his voice soft and even, although the tears continued to roll down his cheeks. I marveled that he could do this. If I were to try to speak while crying, I knew that my speech would be peppered with hiccups and sobs, that my mouth and face would be all distorted and screwed up. "About being unworthy, I mean," he went on. "Over the years, I been wondering what to do about forgiveness. The Bible is all the time saying we should forgive one another. Your mother seems to be able to do it real easy, but I find I'm no good at it at all anymore. Seems to me that even the good Lord Himself wouldn't have wanted us all to just lie down and be walked over."

Zackary was looking at the floor now, his hands clasped tight, eyes dry and moving to and fro, like they were memorizing the pattern on the carpet.

"You have two choices, my boy," said Dad, his words still firm and quiet. "You can stick around and be just what you suggest. You can be one of our hired servants. I should've taken you up on that proposal fourteen years back. You can bake cakes and clean floors and wash dishes and mow lawns and clean all your junk out of the garage. You can paint the house. You can iron your own shirts. You can spread your charm around on a daily basis, instead of saving it up for special occasions."

There was a long silence. I think my dad was breathing hard, or doing whatever it took to get himself under control. Then he started to speak again.

"I hate to bring any more misery into this house than we already have, Zackary, but I'm giving you another choice." He looked hard at Zack, and then he shouted, so that we all jumped, *"Look at me, Zackary!"*

Zackary looked. He looked up from under his lids, and I thought, He looks shifty. He doesn't even look handsome to me anymore. Cheap, I thought. Cheap and shifty.

"If you don't like the first choice," said my dad, his voice quiet again, "there's always the second. You can clear out."

Nothing happened for maybe as long as five minutes, and Zack was staring at the carpet again, eyes darting. Nobody spoke. You could hear Mom sniffling, and from time to time a chain saw somewhere down the street whined, but mostly the silence was just pressing in on our ears. I sat there counting the flowers on the wallpaper so that I wouldn't be able to look at him.

Then Zackary rose and went upstairs to his room. We could hear him moving around up there, shuffling about, opening drawers, thunking things down. In about half an hour, he came down the stairs carrying two suitcases. He stopped at the bottom, and then came over and touched Mom on the shoulder. That's all. Then he just walked out the door without a word.

I grieved a lot after Zack left. I grieved for Lizzie, of course, and I grieved for Mom and Dad, and I grieved for my own broken dream. Zack rode the rails out West, and we heard from Alberta friends that he drifted around the small towns out there, trying this job and that, playing poker, drinking cheap wine, always moving on.

I think Mom saw the justice of what Dad did, but I don't think she ever forgave him, either. She lost two children in one week, and that's too many for someone who had only four to begin with. She became senile early—in her late sixties—and she used to sit all day in a chair in the nursing home's common room, with her head drooped over on one side. Her hair was straight and ragged, her eyes open but empty. Her hands would be clasped in front of her, knuckles white, and she'd be forever and ever muttering, "All my fault. All my fault." Or occasionally she'd yell, in a loud tormented voice, "Too late! Too late!" Then the nurses would come running and give her a sedative.

I'm married now, with three children, and I hardly ever think about Zackary anymore. I'm too busy with my own life and my own family. My children are all girls, two of them quiet and sweet, but the third like quicksilver, pretty and mischievous, quick-tempered and full of laughter. Our home revolves around the magic of her personality. She sheds light upon all of us. Her name is Stephanie, and she is thirteen years old. The other day she became angry at something one of her friends had done. Racing into our kitchen, she pushed her two sisters aside, and, seizing a jug of milk from the table, hurled it at the opposite wall. There was a loud crash, and crockery and milk flew in all directions. Then Stephanie sat down on a chair, with her head in her hands. Finally she lifted up her beautiful little face, framed by her long golden hair, and looked up at me from under a fringe of curling lashes.

"Mom, darling," she began, voice faltering, "I'm so sorry. I'm *so, so, so* sorry. I've gone and done it again." She rose from the chair with a familiar grace, and passed her hand across her forehead, sighing. "I can't imagine what came over me. Mom, sweetie. Can you forgive me? I could die with being sorry. Tell me what I can do to make me feel good again. I feel so terrible. I can hardly bear it."

I looked at her, listened to her, and longed to hold her in my arms and whisper consolation. But somewhere in the back of my head, I could hear a voice shouting, "Too late! Too late!"

I looked at Stephanie again. Despite her agonized expression, her eyes were dry. I recalled that these temper tantrums had been pretty frequent of late, as had the moving speeches of regret and apology. I had put it all down to the shifting hormones of a thirteen-year-old, and assumed that the violence would eventually pass. I looked now at the wall. The pitcher had cracked the paint where it had hit, and there was milk from one side of the room to the other. The floor was a lake, and drops of sticky milk were clinging to windows, curtains, kitchen utensils, dishes.

Something else. My two other daughters were watching this drama from the doorway. They were looking at Stephanie and they were studying me. I did not like the look on their faces.

"Stephanie," I began, keeping my voice friendly, "if you want to do something to feel better, I'll help you." She smiled a grateful smile. "I'm going over to Mrs. Vincent's," I continued, "to help her hang her new living room curtains. While I'm gone, I want you to clean up the milk and the broken china. There are rags and a pail at the bottom of the basement stairs. The curtains will have to be washed by hand, because the red dye runs. They're cotton, so you'll have to iron them. You'll also find milk on all those utensils in their container, as well as on most surfaces. Those china jugs are on sale at Zeller's, and I'd like you to take that allowance money you've been saving and go downtown for a new one. We have some green paint left over from when we painted the kitchen, so fortunately you won't have to buy that. You can repaint that wall on Saturday morning. I'll see that no one gets in your way."

Then, lest I weaken at the sight of her stricken face, I tiptoed through the milk and walked out of the kitchen.

"Thank you, Zackary," I said.

"What?" she said.

"Nothing important," I lied, and shut the door behind me.

The Canoe Trip

When Charles and Luke came to say good-bye, Susie was sitting in the rocker feeding the baby.

"Don't push him too hard, Charles," she said, almost shyly. "He's pretty little."

"You don't have to worry, Susie," he said. "You know that. I don't happen to think that pushing hard is what fathers are for."

Charles glanced at her fondly. She looks good feeding babies, he thought—or doing almost anything else, for that matter. But she was wearing that shapeless red dressing gown he hated. Why on earth, he wondered, does she choose to wear something that looks like an old gunnysack, when she could be showing off the marvelous body that she's got underneath? From time to time he suggested that she throw it away.

"I'll buy you another one," he'd beg. "For a nonbirthday present. An expensive one. Blue. Blue would be nice. That soft stuff like velvet. I'd like that. You'd look gorgeous in it."

"Velour," she'd say. "No thanks, Charles. This one's comfortable. I feel like I'm crawling back into a warm womb. Besides, the color cheers me up." She clung to it like a Linus blanket. And of course he didn't press it. He was not into nagging. That had been his father's territory. He felt a tension in his forehead and rubbed it, horizontally, with the fingers of his left hand.

Charles smiled down at his son. Luke looked like a carbon copy of himself—stocky and square, with an unmanageable mop of curly black hair. He was eight years old. The kid still had arms and legs that were straight and spindly, but Charles knew that in ten years he'd be built for moving pianos.

Dressed in a set of oilskins, Luke gazed up at his father from under his sou'wester with naked worship. They were dressed in identical suits—Luke's brand new and shining yellow, Charles's spotted and faded from a decade of canoe trips.

With some concern, Charles looked out the window at the steady drizzle; but the Bedford weather office had promised sun before eleven. The clock in the hall rang six o'clock. Only five more hours, maybe less. And it was clear from Luke's face that he wouldn't care if the heavens opened and poured forth locusts. This was his first canoe trip.

They'd been out in the canoe a number of times before—three times, maybe more. Charles had explained and demonstrated all the basic skills of paddling, and little by little, he had let Luke try out the different bow strokes. All had been harmony and pleasure. Charles had felt a dual reaction to all of this—pride in his own wise parenting, and an aching regret for those early expeditions with his father. As though it had happened an hour ago or yesterday, he could hear that exasperated voice: "My God, Charles, surely you could have avoided that rock!"; "Keep your eyes open! The bowsman can't relax his vigilance for one second. You're paddling like a dreaming girl!"; "Tired? Don't be ridiculous, son! Being tired is part of the sport. Be a man!"

All he could remember about those early canoe trips was fear, arms like numb stumps, a smoking anger deep in his chest. Only when he finally went to Y Camp did he discover the pride and delight of canoeing. It took until then to realize that rivers wound through peaceful woods and flowered meadows, that birds sang above the water, that rabbits, squirrels, deer watched from the slippery banks.

Charles kissed the top of Susie's head, and touched the baby's cheek. "Your two men will be home by six, for sure," he said. "Maybe earlier. You can pick us up at Brown's Lake bridge, and we'll get my car tomorrow." He smiled at her. "Have a good day without us. There's a sale on at Eaton's. You might like to go. They're selling off . . . dressing gowns."

"It'll take more than bribery to get me out of this beloved garment," Susie said, pulling its soft warmth around her against the chill of the May morning. She smiled. "Have fun. Sure you've got the can opener? Matches?"

"Luke's in charge of both those things. Okay, son? Nothing forgotten or left behind?"

Luke pulled a crumpled piece of paper out of his pocket and studied it slowly, carefully. He grinned at his father. "All set. All systems go."

On the way to Smythe's Landing, Luke fell asleep, and Charles drove through the early morning with deep satisfaction. The soft drizzle intensified the lushness of the countryside. "My son and I," Charles whispered to himself. He visualized himself and Luke, year after year, setting out in companionable peace to explore the river systems, to ski the woods, to hike through miles of wilderness—bush crashing, traveling by compass, blazing trails. He saw them standing together beside quiet streams, casting flies into the water, reeling in fish after fish, cooperating in the business of landing and netting. And today was the launching.

An hour and a half later, as they drove down into the valley, Charles could see the gray river winding its way through the foggy woods. His chest knotted with excitement. When he finally reached Smythe's Landing, he slowed the car to a stop and poked Luke in the ribs. "Up and out, Luke," he said. "Pick up as much gear as you can, and put it down on the dock. I'll get the rest."

Still groggy with sleep, Luke started hauling stuff out of the car. Twice he dropped things. Three times he tripped over a stump or a branch. Once he fell.

Looks like me, Charles mused, but lacks my coordination. Takes after his mother, who can stumble over a feather. Lovable but clumsy—both of them.

However, Charles said nothing—as, indeed, he had carefully said nothing when Luke had dropped countless balls, failed to reach first base, lost minnow after minnow as he struggled to bait hooks, seemed unable to move with any kind of speed or grace. *Time. It just takes time. And patience.*

Today would be different. During Charles's description of the various paddling skills, Luke had shown remarkable understanding of the principles underlying the various strokes. And in the course of their few practice sessions on Maynard's Lake, he had done very well. He was also a willing and amiable helper. And intelligent.

"Dad."

"Yes?"

"I'm wet. There's rain crawling down my neck."

"It's part of the sport, son. Pull down your hat and yank up your collar. Can't expect to be bone dry in a rainstorm." The drizzle had increased to a full driving rain, and the canoe was slippery as they stowed their gear inside it.

"How many miles, Dad?" Luke asked as he adjusted himself in the bow.

"Just ten. A real short trip."

They pushed off. As the canoe moved smoothly out into the river, Charles experienced yet again the warm anticipation that attended the start of all canoe expeditions.

"Dad."

"What?"

"Can I change sides?"

"Not tired already?"

"Yes. Kind of. How much farther?"

"We've only gone a few hundred yards, Luke. We've got a long way to go. On my first canoe trip, my father and I went twenty-five miles."

There was a sound from the bow.

"What was that you said, son?"

"Nothing."

They rounded a bend, and Charles glimpsed a heron standing watch over the river on a submerged rock, silhouetted against the misty trees.

"Psst! Look!" Charles whispered.

"What, Dad?" Luke yelled. "I can't hear you."

Charles sighed as the startled heron left the rock and disappeared behind a group of spruce trees.

"Never mind. It's too late."

During the next hour, the rain increased. Charles scanned the sky in vain for some sort of opening in the cloud cover. So it was Luke who saw the mother duck and her four ducklings crossing the river. He turned around abruptly in his seat and waved his paddle, face wide open with joy.

"Hey! Look, Dad! Look!"

"Righto, Luke. Terrific. But listen. You can't leap around like that in a canoe. It's not a stable craft. They tip. Like *easily*. We could be in the water in nothing flat. Sorry, but that's just the way it is. Next time, just *tell* me."

They paddled on in silence. Every so often, Luke would point to something—a chipmunk, a beaver dam, an unusual flower, a rock that looked like a serpent. Charles mentioned things of beauty, of interest, of amusement. A perfect day, thought Charles.

"Dad."

"Yes?"

"Don't we ever stop?"

"Why? What do you mean, 'stop'?"

"Like *stop*. You know. Stop paddling."

"But we're on a trip, not a picnic. Wait till you're so tired you feel like you'll die if you do one more stroke."

"Dad."

"Yes?"

"That's how I feel."

Charles looked at his watch. And at the riverbank.

"Look, Luke, there just isn't any place we can stop right now. There's a great spot farther on where I'd planned to have lunch. Can you hang on till then? Maybe a couple of hours?"

23

Mutter from the bow.

"What?"

"Nothing."

My God, Charles thought, looking at the drenched figure in the bow, his small hands grasping the paddle, *he's so little.*

"Listen, Luke. Can you hear me?"

"Yeah."

"Stop paddling. I'll go it alone for a while."

"Okay, Dad."

"But look. Can you stop wiggling? Try to sit still."

"My foot's gone to sleep."

"Well listen, then, try to ease down, and see if you can sit on the bottom of the canoe for a while."

Watching Luke ease down took stamina. He seemed to have at least four legs, and neither of his arms appeared to be performing any valuable function. Charles grabbed the sides of the canoe and stabilized it, as Luke maneuvered himself onto the bottom.

"Good. Now, rest."

Charles discovered that it was just as easy to paddle the canoe now as it had been when Luke had been helping. *Lily Dipper.* Charles heard this phrase from way back, twenty-five years ago: "Anyone who's got no more push on their paddle than that is nothing but a damn Lily Dip-per." And "For God's sake, Charles, try to get a little more heft into your stroke!"

"Having fun, son?" He smiled at Luke.

"Sure. Great." He was hunched over, hugging himself.

"Cold?"

"A bit. It's okay."

Charles paddled on for the next hour. Would the rain never stop? He was sorry Luke was cold and wet, but by gosh, so was he. And the expedition was for Luke, after all. He was a patient and uncomplaining kid, but he wasn't exactly radiating rousing good cheer. Charles wondered if perhaps he wasn't demanding enough of him. Too hard was bad, but maybe too soft was worse.

"Up you get, son, and let's have some work out of you. I need your help."

"Sure, Dad. I'm fine now."

Charles had forgotten about the hazards of Luke moving around in a canoe. His blade, flattened on the water, just barely saved them from a spill, as Luke heaved his body from the floor onto the bow seat.

Another hour and it was time for lunch. Charles beached the canoe and saw a tree where they might find some shelter. Then he hauled the heaviest knapsack out of the craft, while Luke labored up and down the bank with smaller items. Water was pouring off their sou'westers and dripping off their noses.

"A good fire will take the chill out of our bones," Charles called out from the shore. "Get out the matches, while I get the bag of kindling and paper. We'll have the soup hot in no time."

When Charles reached the place he had picked out for lunch, he noted with satisfaction that it was almost dry. The pine tree was high and thick, and the ground was level and carpeted with pine needles. Then he saw Luke's face— white, bleak, *scared*.

"What's up, son? You'll be okay in a minute. Let's have the matches."

Luke just stood there dripping, motionless. Then: "They're not here," he said. "The bag's not here . . . That means the can opener, too."

"Luke." Charles spoke carefully. Mustn't spoil every- thing. "That stuff was your responsibility. I told you to pack it. And to check."

"I did pack it, Dad. And I checked it, too. The bag was in the car. But I don't even remember what I carried down to the canoe."

Charles's mind slid over the memory of Luke's sleep-walking exit from the car, stumbling, falling, eyes barely open. That hot soup was taking on all the appeal of a barbecued steak.

"We've got some bread and peanut butter, Luke," he said. "No doubt we can survive on that." He could hear the edge in his voice.

Charles toyed with the idea of making a lark of their deprivation, of pretending to be pioneers surviving on pemmican. But then he thought, To hell with it. I'm too wet to care. Besides, it won't hurt him to find out that his errors won't always be greeted with a smile. Granted you can't build a man in a day, but you can start laying a few bricks. They ate their sandwiches in silence under the tree.

That afternoon they paddled three more hours. The rain stopped, but a stiff breeze came up from the north, and the going was hard. Charles struggled against the wind, while the Lily Dipper slogged along—in, out, in, out—without rhythm, out of phase, contributing nothing. Exhausted, Charles scraped his thumb against the side of the canoe, and he could see the blood starting to flow. Reaching forward to his knapsack, he dug into the front pocket for his first-aid kit. A Band-Aid wouldn't make it stop hurting, but it could keep him from spilling blood all over his gear. The kit wasn't there. It was inconceivable that it was not, but in the excitement of his departure, he must have forgotten to get it out of the car's glove compartment. It had been on his own list, carefully compiled with Luke's assistance. Maybe it had been Luke's job to get it. A part of him clung to this tempting idea.

He pulled a handkerchief out of his pocket and wound it around his thumb, tying it securely.

"You okay, Dad?"

"Yeah. Yeah, sure."

Sure. Wonderful. Wet, frozen to death, totally bushed, and to all intents and purposes, stark alone.

At last, mercifully, there was only about a quarter of a mile left to go. The sun had come bursting through the trees and the wind had died down. Just around that bend would be the bridge, where Susie would be waiting with a warm car and three dry daughters. Daughters. He could maybe try taking Colleen next time. She was big for her age, tough and spirited. There wasn't any law that said it had to be a *son* who went on canoe trips. He'd not had any sisters, and he still thought of little girls as made of sugar and spice, of material that lacked what his father used to call *fiber*.

Thunk! They hit a rock, and the canoe spun around.

The woods, the sky, the slithering river exploded with Charles's voice.

"Goddammit, Luke! Didn't you see that rock? That's what a bowsman's *for!* You can't take your eyes off the water for one *second!* It's not like you're any damn use as a paddler. You could at least use your *eyes!* Am I supposed to do every goddamn thing myself?"

Luke swung around and stared at his father, eyes round, mouth open.

"Turn around, you little fool!" Charles yelled. "And see if just for once you can do it carefully. Try, just *try* not to be so fucking clumsy! And *paddle!* There're rocks ahead, in case you didn't notice, and we have to get around them fast!"

Luke dug into the water with frenzied speed and zero control. His whole body was shaking, and the water splashed around his paddle as though he were throwing lumber into the river. Miraculously, they avoided the rapids, and Charles steered the canoe to a sandy beach, just their side of the bend. Beyond the point was the bridge and Susie's car full of daughters. He wasn't ready for them yet.

When the canoe came to a standstill by the beach, Luke sat like a statue, a small waxwork figure clad in yellow oilskins. Charles hung on to a tree that reached over the water; he leaned his forehead against the trunk and contemplated the empty cave that was the center of his chest. Eight years of trying to be a perfect father, and in less than a minute, he'd blown the entire thing. He could see his father sitting on the riverbank at the end of one of their canoe trips. He had been tall, lean, and immensely strong, and he was sitting on the grass with his head in his hands, tears streaming down his face. Charles had always assumed they'd been tears of anger and disappointment, after yet another frustrating trip—despair over a son who had failed once again to live up to his expectations.

As Charles sat there, gazing at his memory, he watched Luke drop his paddle in the river and fall out of the canoe.

They were close to the shore. There was no danger. Even the paddle was safe. But by the time he had fished Luke out of the water, laid him on the shore, and secured the canoe and the paddles, Charles's body was trembling like a poplar branch. Luke was sitting up on the wet grass, shivering, eyes staring straight ahead.

Charles stumbled back up the bank and wrapped his own coat around Luke. Taking him in his arms, rocking him back and forth on his lap, like a baby, he moaned over and over again, "Oh my son, my son, my son."

After a long time, he stopped rocking, and both their bodies were still. Charles cleared his throat and said, "Are you okay, Luke?"

"Yes, Dad."

"Are you sure?"

"Yes." Then, "Are *you?*"

Charles closed his eyes. He didn't answer. Then he said, "That wasn't you I was yelling at back there, you know."

"No."

"Oh, hell," Charles sighed. "I can't expect you to understand. How else can I put it?"

"But I do."

"Do what?"

"Understand. I did it last week." As he spoke, he fiddled with his father's shirt buttons.

"Did what?"

"What you just did. I got mad at Harvey because I was mad at something else. I yelled at him and threw a rock right through a basement window in that empty house on Hawthorne Street."

Harvey was Luke's best friend. Charles had never seen them exchange so much as a cross word.

"But when I'm with you, you're always so quiet and polite. How come?"

"Because that's the way you want me to be."

Charles passed his hand across his eyes. "You must have been pretty wild when you let fly at Harvey. What was the matter?"

"Oh, I dunno." Luke stopped fidgeting with the buttons and clasped his hands together in his lap. The sun was starting to dry his matted hair, his wet face.

"What? Tell me."

"Well . . ."

"C'mon, Luke. Let's have it."

"Well. You. It was you I was mad at."

"Me! For what?"

"For yacking at Mom. You're all the time bugging her about that red dressing gown. I think it's really pretty. She looks cool in it. She likes it." He paused. "So I got mad."

Then Luke spoke again. "I'm sorry I spoiled your trip. I know you weren't yelling those awful things *really* at me, but I know I spoiled your trip."

My trip.

"You didn't, Luke. The weather did. *I* did. I should have planned a shorter trip. I should have let you practice more. I shouldn't have expected you to be eighteen years old. I'm the dumb one, not you. I don't know how to tell you this—how to fix it."

Luke stood up and grinned. "You don't have to," he said. "You just did." Charles held out his large brown hand, and Luke stretched out his thin arm. They shook hands. They looked at each other.

"I love you," Charles said.

"Me too, Dad," said Luke. "A whole lot."

Susie, the baby, and the two little girls were waiting at the bridge. As the car climbed the hill away from Brown's Lake, Charles turned around and looked down the steep hill.

"Look, Luke," he said.

In the distance the wet forest shone in the evening sun. The river was a dazzling ribbon of light moving through the valley below. A look of complete understanding passed between them.

On the way home, Luke talked for thirty minutes about the ducks, the beaver dams, the picnic in the rain, the hazardous rocks, the chipmunk. Then he fell asleep until they reached their house an hour later.

"Well," said Susie that night, as she and Charles prepared for bed, "was it as great as you expected?"

Charles thought a moment before he answered. "Better," he said.

"Why? It was a pretty crummy day."

"Well, because among other things—among a whole lot of other things—it was the day I forgave my father."

"Oh?" She waited for more.

"Sometime I may tell you about it. Maybe. Maybe not."

Susie didn't press him. "Okay," she said. She was sitting at her dressing table in her slip, unfastening her earrings.

"One more thing," said Charles.

"What's that?"

"That red dressing gown . . ."

"Uh huh?"

"Keep it. Enjoy it." He grinned. "Money to buy a new one is from this moment withdrawn."

"Sometimes," muttered Susie, as she disappeared into the bathroom for her shower, "I don't even begin to understand men."

The Dandelion garden

A Modern Fable for Elderly Children

In a land not far away and not so long ago, a son was born to two people of humble means. Although low in funds, the father was high in pretensions, and named his son Hamlet. "For," he explained, "this is no ordinary boy. He is our firstborn, and I intend that he shall be profound and inscrutable and undeniably great."

Hamlet displayed a notable lack of profundity during the first five years of his life. He did all the usual things. This pleased his father, who, like all parents, regarded usual things as unusual when performed by his own child. He developed remarkable and miraculous skills: he learned how to unbutton his shoes, to go to the bathroom, to throw a ball, to catch beetles, and to color between the lines. "Clearly," said the father, as he watched this singular development from nothing to something, "this is no ordinary child."

Then, in the spring of one memorable year, Hamlet had his fifth birthday. On the day after his birthday, when he was just five years and twenty-four hours old, he took a spade into the garden, with the intention of increasing his collection of beetles. Upon entering the garden, however, he stopped short, with one of his legs suspended two inches from the ground. He dropped his spade, as the delight of his discovery drained the strength from his arms. He sat down so that he might survey the miracle at closer range. The lawn was a lawn no longer. It was a sea of sunshine, and the flowers that made up the infinity of yellowness were everywhere. When he recovered from the initial shock, Hamlet snatched one of the flowers from its stem and rushed into the house.

"What is it?" he demanded of his mother, thrusting the flower before her eyes.

"A dandelion, of course," said his mother, looking at the flower with distaste.

He hardly dared ask the next question. At last he summoned the courage. "Is it strong?" he asked nervously. "Will it grow easily?"

His mother searched about in her mind for an adjective capable of describing the gargantuan strength of dandelions. Finally she resorted to the force of simplicity and gave her answer. "*Very*," she replied.

The boy's relief was enormous. For a moment it was enough to know that the flowers would endure and come again. But soon the desire to possess the object of his love overcame him. "Could I," he faltered. "May I . . . *take* some?"

"Please, do," said his mother with feeling, and disappeared upstairs to make the beds.

Beetles were forgotten. So also were balls, swings, crayons, and Sunday-school picnics. He applied himself with concentration and devotion and toil and delicacy to the planting of a dandelion garden. He chose a spot at the back of the yard behind the hedge, where he might work unnoticed and undisturbed. "I'm making a surprise, I'm making a surprise," he chanted over and over to himself, as he thrust his spade into the earth; then he made up a little tune to go with the words. He dug up the plants one by one from the lawn, removing each one with such care that not a leaf was harmed. This took a long time. Next he made a soft roomy hole, deposited the plant, sprinkled it with fertilizer, and watered it carefully, generously, and accurately. Then he patted it lovingly into the ground. By the end of two weeks, he had forty-two plants in his garden. He was satisfied. The display was adequate in numbers and very splendid in effect. It was five o'clock, and he was tired.

He chose his mother first. He chose her because he loved her, and also because there was no one else around at the time. He dashed, he tore, he flew into the kitchen, and, pulling at his mother's apron, gasped, "Come! Come! Come quickly to the garden and see my surprise!"

Hamlet's mother paused for a moment in the middle of her preparations for the evening meal. She looked at him and failed to notice the visionary glitter in his eyes. "Your face," she said, "is dirty. Go wash and tidy yourself before going any further."

Washed and combed, he returned, still aglow. "Come with me," he begged. "Come. Please. To the garden."

"Not now," she said, puncturing the balloon of his delight. "I have no time. I must peel the potatoes, heat the water, scrape the carrots, pour the milk, set the table, whip the cream, cook the meat, sweep the floor, and change my clothes before dinner. Tomorrow I will come. Not now. I have no time."

Hamlet shivered. But he answered, because he had no choice, "Yes, Mother, we will go tomorrow."

The next day, the dandelions were wilted and bent. Even dandelions will not last indefinitely, and their season was past. "Next year," said the boy, "is forever. But I will wait and build another garden in another spring, and this time I will take my father to see it. He will come."

The year passed, another spring arrived, and Hamlet was six. At the first appearance of the dandelions, he started to work with great haste. This time he planted his garden with even more care, arranging the flowers in special groups, curves, and circles. It took him two weeks to complete it, and when it was done he stood back and surveyed it with joy and with pride.

He had learned something the previous year. He washed his hands and face carefully, and waited for the right moment to approach his father. When his father seemed comfortably occupied in doing nothing at all, Hamlet walked quickly up to him.

"Father," he began. "Father, please come with me. I have a surprise to show you—a fine thing I have made all by myself. It has taken me two weeks to finish it." He pulled at his father's arm.

"Fine, my son," said his father, already guessing at the nature of the surprise. It would be a tree house, a handmade steam engine, or a car fashioned from orange crates. Truly,

Hamlet was a remarkably creative child. He followed his son into the backyard.

Hamlet was overwhelmed by his father's willingness to come. He could bear the suspense no longer. "Father," he cried, "my surprise is a dandelion garden!"

His father stopped walking. "A garden?" he thought, with deep dismay. "My son, my firstborn—a wimp!" He turned to his son in anger, and then checked himself. "This is a problem of great delicacy," he argued to himself. "As a wise father, I will handle it with control and with calm." Thus he congratulated himself.

"Let us have a little talk, first," said his father, placing a hand upon Hamlet's shoulder. Despite the warmth of the afternoon, Hamlet could feel a chilly wind on the back of his neck. "All right, Father," he replied, his eyes fastened upon the hedge.

"Boys," said the father, "are different from girls. They like climbing trees and building boats and throwing balls and playing marbles and going fishing and making forts and having snowball fights. Boys are not interested in flowers. Sometimes men plant gardens, but this is in order to improve the value of their property. Your mother is calling us in to dinner." Then his father, in a generous welling-up of understanding and wisdom, once more placed his hand upon Hamlet's shoulder. "I'm sure," he concluded, "that we understand one another."

That evening Hamlet looked lovingly at his garden. He already possessed it, but now the desire to share it with someone else was a flood straining to be loosed. Tomorrow he would find that person.

But the next day was the fifteenth day, and it was too late. The garden was no longer in full bloom, and there is nothing sadder than a withered flower. "Next year," sighed Hamlet, "is forever and ever, but I will make another garden and show it to a gardener. A gardener is a lover of flowers and will understand."

The leaves fell and the snow passed, and it was spring again. In greatest secrecy, Hamlet planted his garden, more intricate and magnificent than ever before. On the fourteenth day, he gazed upon the blooms and knew that this was more beautiful than the other gardens. The dandelions were tall and strong; their blooms were like the rays of the sun; the design of their arrangement was marvelous to see. He went forth in search of a gardener.

"Gardener," he said when he finally found one, "I have made a garden. Will you come to see it?"

"Good," exclaimed the gardener. "I would like very much to see your garden. No doubt the flowers are very beautiful. I trust that you have eliminated all the weeds."

"What is a weed?" asked Hamlet.

"A weed," said the gardener, "is a very terrible thing, and the worst kind of weed is a dandelion. It tries hard to grow in every flower garden. It even invades the lawns. Everyone knows that each blade of grass must be rescued from the ravages of a dandelion. I have in my pocket a very effective weed-killer. Since you are interested in gardens, you may have this bottle. Sprinkle a little on every dandelion tonight, and by morning each one will be twisted and wilted and completely dead. Now—take me to see your garden."

The gardener looked around in surprise. The boy was gone. He shrugged his shoulders and returned to his job of grafting two rare rosebushes.

It was six o'clock now, and too late for Hamlet to find someone else before the dawning of the fifteenth day. He spent the evening watering his garden. He wore a heavy sweater, because he felt very cold.

And so it came to pass that each year Hamlet spent two weeks making a dandelion garden. Every year it was finer than it had been the year before. On the fourteenth day he always looked for one person with whom he could share it.

One year he asked a schoolteacher to come and admire

his blooms. "How long has it taken you to tend this garden?" she asked.

"Two weeks," he replied.

"And how much time have you spent on arithmetic and spelling and history and geography and grammar?" she inquired.

"Not much time at all," he answered. "But a dandelion is a wonderful thing. You can lick the end of it and make the stem curl into a hundred different curves and wiggles."

"That," she said, "is of no educational value, and is therefore of no significance."

He spoke one spring to a businessman of great wealth and prominence. "This is an idle way to spend your time, my boy," said the man. "You must apply yourself to life in a practical way, collecting enough knowledge and skill to make yourself wealthy and important."

"But," argued Hamlet, "a dandelion is a very useful thing. When it has gone to seed you can blow the seeds away and find out what time it is."

"Ah," sighed the man, "but you may blow the wrong number of times, and therefore be confused as to the correct time. To a man of business, the correct time is of prime importance. The reason you give for valuing a dandelion is of no significance at all."

The Dandelion Garden

A clergyman admonished him for spending his time in a useless way, asking if he had done any good works or said any prayers during the two-week interval. Hamlet could recall neither good works nor prayers. However, he replied, "Dandelions can be used for good purposes. You can poke holes in their stems, put other dandelions in the holes, weave them together, and make a flower chain. This can be presented as a gift to one's grandmother, to place about her neck."

"This is a very frivolous purpose," replied the clergyman, "and cannot be regarded as of any significance."

Finally he found an artist. "Surely," he felt, "she will come to see my garden and will marvel at its great beauty."

"Most flowers are lovely," she told him, "but if there is any flower that can be regarded as commonplace, it is the dandelion. Why do you not plant roses?"

"But the dandelion is the first flower of the year," he replied, "and it is also of a perfect and symmetrical form."

"It matters not at all if a flower arrives in May or December," she argued, "and besides, a dandelion is too perfect. Were I to paint a field of dandelions, I could put dabs of yellow paint at random throughout the grass on my picture, and everyone would say, 'Yes, those are dandelions.'

But were I to paint a rose, I would have to paint each petal with infinite care."

Hamlet did not bother to reply. Her arguments, he felt, were of no significance at all. Besides, he was tired. He was tired of arguing, tired of searching, tired of planting. He was, in fact, tired of being young. He was eleven years old that spring.

The next year an old man came wandering through the land. No one knew where he came from or where he was going, but he seemed to be looking for someone. Finally he reached the town in which Hamlet lived. It was the fifteenth day of the garden, and Hamlet was sitting by the hedge, building a steam engine out of soup cans.

"I have been looking for you," said the man. "I am a dandelion grower. I am a hundred and ninety-nine years old and I have spent my life in the cultivation and care of dandelions. I have twenty-two acres of land on which are planted eighty-eight million dandelions. Every year I go on a long journey, searching for one other person with whom I can share my flowers. You are the person."

With listless eyes, Hamlet looked up at the man. "It is too late," he replied. "I used to be a grower of dandelions myself, but now I am a builder of steam engines. I am twelve years old, and I now know that the cultivation of dandelions is an unmanly pursuit. Dandelions are useless, time-consuming, frivolous, and much too common. Besides, they are weeds. Last night I, too, returned from my search for a person with whom to share my garden. Finding myself unsuccessful for the eighth time, I came back home and in great wrath stamped upon my flowers until they were all dead. I am twelve years old now, and very wise, and a maker of steam engines." The boy looked at him with such fierce determination that the old man knew it was useless to argue. He turned away from Hamlet and wept.

So Hamlet grew up to be a very efficient and successful engineer. By developing a habit of averting his eyes when in the presence of dandelions, he became moderately content; indeed, in the course of time, he grew to be quite fond of engines and machines and bridges and dams. His father, of course, was both relieved and delighted by this turn of events. Nobody knows what became of the old man. There were not even any rumors, because no one was very interested. However, you may have noticed that dandelions are, if anything, on the increase. This fact may be of some significance.

On the other hand, it may mean nothing at all.

Cordelia Clark

Charlie, my friend, let's have a little talk. I feel a story coming over me. An old and miserable story. About me.

A lot of people may think it's pretty weird to carry on a running conversation with a dog. Were I sixteen instead of seventy-six, I'd probably feel the same way. At sixteen, intriguing conversations are not difficult to come by—at school, at parties, on the beach, in the mall. But at seventy-six, the ranks of interesting conversationalists are dwindling. Strokes, Charlie, general lassitude, death. So the urge to deliver monologues becomes more and more attractive. Especially now that my husband is gone. And dogs, unlike a lot of people, are excellent listeners.

I have always loved the name Charlie; why, I don't

know. But I'm so attached to the name that I call all my dogs Charlie. Over the years, I've had fifteen of them.

There are those who find this Charlie fixation ghoulish. If your dog is dead, they say, bury him, forget him, and get on with the dance. Well, I'm dancing, aren't I? I always get a new dog within a month of the burying, but that's not to say that I can just fill up the hole in my heart left by the old one. The dog is new, and within a day I love him, but the name is a link, a connection, to a lot of happy memories.

So, male or female, the dog is always Charlie. And it's really nobody's business but my own.

Nor do I much care what people think about most other things, either. That is one of the blessings connected to age—I'm not saying *old age,* because I don't think that this need become a real factor before one is, say, eighty-five. Not if your genes are good, and if you eat lots of fiber, and go for a long walk every day. And to be freed from caring what people think is such a relief, Charlie, such a release from the Knotted Stomach Syndrome, that I'm sure that those of us who achieve it can add at least five years to our life expectancies.

But I was not always blessed with this ability to disregard the opinions of others. And I will have to admit, Charlie, if I'm being totally honest, that I'm still more vulnerable in this area than I like to think. While shopping in the mall yesterday, I found myself wondering, with real anxiety, why Mr. Zwitz was looking so intently at my hair, and why that deep groove had formed between his eyebrows. Nervously, I touched my head, I patted it—little ineffectual pats. And then, passing a mirror in the mall, I caught sight of myself. As straight as a stick (my hair) and lying every which way (and sparsely) on my pink scalp. That meant that I'd forgotten to curl it, which also meant that I'd left the curling iron plugged into the wall, switched to the ON button.

I left the mall in considerable haste, my shopping not even half completed, telling myself that I must dash home to prevent that curling iron from burning up my end table and eventually my entire house. But deep inside, Charlie, I knew that the real reason for my haste was a kind of fear. I didn't want anyone else looking at me with that degree of distaste and (probably) pity. Talking to your dog is one thing; looking like a witch is quite another. For the fact is that I'm regarded as being remarkably well preserved for a woman of seventy-six, and it matters to me that this is so. I could visualize Mr. Zwitz hustling up to that perky-looking Krystal Curtis in the post office and whispering (or worse still, just *saying*), "I saw Trudy Bergen in the mall today. She's obviously failing." Failing at what, I wonder. At life? At prettiness? At looking young for my age? At dignity, I think. Failing. A terrible term, with connotations I dare not dwell on.

But never mind, Charlie. That sort of reaction on my part is rare, these days. My behavior is almost always free-wheeling and confident. I'm open and sure about my political opinions, my ongoing discourse with St. Anthony, my friendships with socially unacceptable people ("Unsuitable," my mother would have said), and my preference for dandelions over roses in my small backyard.

I remember my earliest years as a time in which everything seemed to be colored yellow. Hence, I speak of my young and yellow days—bright and warm and altogether pleasant.

The gray days, the black days, the days that were spiky and coarse, those days commenced with the arrival in our neighborhood of Cordelia Clark.

I cannot expect you to be aware of this irony, Charlie, but Cordelia happens to have been the only one of King Lear's daughters who truly loved him—with a love that was ill-expressed and exceedingly unwise. Nor can you know about the resulting misery of both their lives, or the agony that separated them. Unlike others I could mention, she did have a short time in which to savor their eventual reunion; but in no time at all, the king carried her onto the stage as dead as a rag doll. All that love—so absolute, so uncompromising, so dangerous.

If, however, in 1927, someone had carried into my presence the lifeless body of Cordelia Clark, age twelve, I would have been hard put to resist offering up a prayer of thanksgiving, followed by a resounding cheer. That is because, Charlie, as far as I could see, she had devoted the entire previous year to my destruction.

There are various ways, Charlie, to destroy people. You can actually kill them outright (knife, gun, a judicious push over a cliff). Or you can destroy something much more subtle, much more difficult to protect than one's life. Cordelia Clark chose this latter route, and her victim was me.

When I was eleven years old, my family lived in a sleepy little town in the Annapolis Valley. The summers were warm, and much sunnier than on the Fundy Shore, a very short distance away. The winters were snowy and crisp, spared the slush and raw mists of Nova Scotia's coastal areas. In the town were large wooden houses, brightly painted, usually in white, with a profusion of Victorian trim in black or dark green. Three churches dominated Main Street, all of them well attended. Poverty, where it existed, was scarcely visible. Gardens nearly always bloomed lavishly in summer, nurtured by a combination of rich soil and almost perfect weather—sunny by day, with the occasional convenient shower by night. How could anything but happiness flourish in such an environment?

Cordelia Clark sailed into town with her parents in one of the first luxury cars to be owned by anyone in Wolfville. The Clark car was a marvel. It was a McLaughlin Buick, large and enclosed, with real doors. Its black dignity was enhanced by its dazzling lacquer finish.

The town was small, so a crowd of curious people appeared almost immediately, as if by magic, to observe this spectacle. The watching crowd even contained dignified ladies who, under normal circumstances, would have avoided staring at anything at all (the stumbling gait of the town drunk, gushing fire hydrants, the sound of a woman's scream from an upstairs window), as they glided along, eyes front, their faces under tight control.

Not so with the arrival of the Clark McLaughlin Buick. The ladies stayed on the outskirts of the crowd, but they were there, looking. Horses shied, possibly portending the direction their lives were to take. More probably, just objecting to the extraordinary noise—the rumbling engine, the squealing children. The men crossed their arms in front of their chests and tried to look knowledgeable about such things. The women whispered behind their gloved hands.

When the car carrying Mr. and Mrs. Clark and their only child, Cordelia (age eleven), finally chugged to a halt, Mr. Eisner, the mayor of the town, stepped forward, and said, with a perfect mixture of dignity and warmth, "Welcome to Wolfville."

Mr. Clark was small-boned and short, dapper, expensively clad, absurdly erect, his thin hair parted in the middle and plastered down on each side of his scalp. As he approached Mr. Eisner, he swaggered, if one can be said to swagger over so short a distance. His chin was held up higher than would be regarded as either attractive or wise in Wolfville, and the hand he held out to the mayor was limp and white, as smooth and as hairless as a woman's. Among the spectators in the crowd, the eyes of the men were unreadable, but they clasped their chests a little tighter with their folded arms, and their own chins rose ever so slightly, almost in unison.

"Inherited money," said Morley Jackson out of the corner of his mouth to Harry Atherton. It was as plain as the nose on your face that Mr. Clark had never done a lick of work in his life.

Then his wife emerged from the car, Charlie—a sight for all to behold. Her clothes would have passed muster at any civic or national event in New York City, or possibly in Boston, where things in general tended to be a little more subdued. In Wolfville, they were at least three seasons ahead of what you could expect to see moving in and out of the post office, or parading in front of the Baptist church. She looked extravagantly fashionable in her dropped waist, short skirt, skinny shoes, silk stockings, and a small black cloche that framed her exquisitely pretty and unsmiling face. She also looked almost imperceptibly vulgar, or possibly simply different from everybody else I was used to seeing. But the mixture of exotic and vulgar was not unpleasing to me. I found it hard to take my eyes off her high-heeled, pointy-toed shoes. I knew they would produce a quick and snappy *click-click-click* when she walked.

But the watching women—I could tell—felt an instant shock of fear. They knew in a flash that this young and lovely woman had married for money. She had wed that unattractive and arrogant man in order to put those expensive clothes on her back, to load her fingers down with diamonds, to ride around in that shiny black McLaughlin Buick. And her eyes were roving. Her glance slid off the

startled clatch of women on the outskirts of the crowd—
already grouping closer together for protection. Her attention settled on the haphazard gathering of men in the
forefront, with their broad Valley faces scorning her husband and assessing every aspect of her own tiny but oddly
voluptuous person. She smiled a crooked smile, looking at
the group out of the corner of her eyes, her head tilted. All
of this happened very quickly, but not before my own eyes
had taken in all of it.

Charlie, grown-ups tend to think that children are deaf
to nuances, wily bits of meanness, sexual undertones. At
the age of seventy-six, Charlie, I'm sometimes guilty of this
myself—this tendency to underestimate the perceptions of
children. Yesterday, after my retreat from Mr. Zwitz and
the mall, I went home and very carefully curled my hair.
Later that day, in the selfsame mall, I met that outspoken
son of Natalie Burgess's. He said to me, he actually did,
Charlie, "Sure looks better. Bet you hope Mr. Zwitz is still
around to see." I wouldn't have believed that a child of that
age could have so accurately read my mind. But I should
have realized. Children's eyes are open very wide indeed,
and their minds are forever ticking away, processing the
data.

So, yes, way back then, I took in all those little subtleties in the colorful arrival of the Clarks. And listened intently when my mother and her friends discussed it the next day, over tea and biscuits and their cross-stitch embroidery.

But I haven't told you about Cordelia. I wanted first to set up a picture of the loins from which she sprang. After her mother's exit from the car, Cordelia stepped out—small, like her parents, with her father's arrogance and her mother's awareness of power written all over her sharp little face, with its direct and daring eyes, its pert nose, its unreadable mouth. She was dressed in a velvet suit with a cameo pin at her neck—hot for this sweltering July day, but there were clearly things more important to Cordelia than heat. She also wore an astonishing pair of shiny pink patent-leather shoes.

Her gaze traveled down the whole length of the double line of children, looked every one of us squarely in the eye, pausing for a moment at each one, as though assessing our worth or usefulness. Without uttering a word, she exuded a magnetic quality that made every last one of us want to be her friend—her *best* friend, if possible. I felt not a flicker of apprehension. I knew only that I wanted her to like me. Such was her power over all of us that day.

And why, you may ask, Charlie, did the Clarks, with all their wealth and mysterious charisma, choose to move to that little town in the Annapolis Valley? Why weren't they settling in Ottawa, Toronto, New York, Washington? Indeed, Charlie, you may well ask that question. It seemed incredible to me at the time that they should have chosen to live among those green fields, with their rows of apple trees and munching cows, with the long lazy afternoons and warm evenings, heavy with the smell of clover. Surely, bright city lights, large parties with clinking glasses, and the insistent beat of dance music would have been a more fitting backdrop for the Clarks.

There were rumors, of course. He was unwell (cancer, TB, some dread exotic disease, maybe from a posting in India). He was hiding from something (bank robbery, assault—but who would he be strong enough to assault?—embezzlement). He was writing a novel (unlikely, it was felt). He rarely left his huge white turreted house with its three floors of round bay windows. When he did, he never paused to pass the time of day with anyone at the post office or the bank or the duck pond. He just nodded solemnly and continued on his way.

In the following weeks, Mrs. Clark would accept numerous invitations to tea. (The women, although uneasy, didn't want it to show.) She attended these social events with visible boredom, dressed up in one of her apparently limitless number of dresses or suits. Conversation with her was tough going, because she had virtually nothing in common with those corseted women, for whom it was crucial to be markedly respectable and to hold their hormones in check, often even in their own beds. Eventually, my mother said, the women of the town stopped inviting her, because she never asked them back—although certainly it would have been easy for her, equipped as she was with a maid and a gardener, as well as a woman who came in twice a week to help with the cleaning.

So she, too, disappeared from view, although she made frequent visits to Halifax in her flashy car, returning days later with the backseat full of parcels and boxes. She also was seen from time to time leaving the house very late at night. Some who suffered from insomnia had watched (avidly) as she came back home just before first light.

Women started baking pecan pies and strawberry trifle for their husbands, and wearing slightly more makeup than had been their custom. Mrs. Harvey Fielding even followed her husband one evening when he had to work late. His office was on the ground floor, so she was able to see that he was just checking his files and typing up inventory. She watched for a long time, but nothing happened, although she confided to my mother (while I was in the hall, listening) that he kept stroking the phone, a gesture that she thought might signify either hope or indecision. When she saw him reach for his coat, she ran home as fast as her bedroom slippers could take her. By the time Harvey arrived in their bedroom, she was lying safely under the covers, her face turned toward the wall. She was breathing deeply—not exactly a snore, something a lot more attractive. My mother laughed when Mrs. Fielding told her that, and I could hear Mrs. Fielding giggling in the background.

But I'm way ahead of myself, Charlie. On the day of their arrival, when Cordelia finished scrutinizing the welcoming contingent of children, I stepped forward. I knew I was in charge of that spellbound group. They always looked to me for directional signals, and I was equipped with more than my share of self-confidence. Besides, my mother had taught me some of the rules of courtesy and kindness. I also wanted to get in there first.

I walked up to a spot directly in front of her. "I'm Trudy Hutchinson," I said. "Want to come over this afternoon and play?" I said this softly. I didn't want twenty-five children turning up on my doorstep.

She looked at me hard, her face unsmiling but alert. I could sense that she was approving of me. Then she asked, "Where do you live?"

I pointed across the street to a pleasant and well-kept house in the next block. "Over there," I said. "The gray one with the white trim." Then I added, shamelessly, "With the veranda all across the front." Their house had no veranda, just a sunporch. In the July heat of the Annapolis Valley, no one would regard a sunporch as much of an asset.

"Okay," she said, quietly, confidently. "Three o'clock." And turned to follow her mother into the house.

I would have preferred three thirty, but I let that pass. I was going downtown with Effie McFarlane at two o'clock. That wouldn't give me much time to pick out my mother's birthday present or to walk up and down Main Street to watch the Saturday shoppers.

Effie was my best friend. We did our homework together every day. We walked on the dikes overlooking Blomidon, and talked about reproduction. We traded the latest gossip about all our schoolmates, and tried to decide whether we liked boys or hated them. When the whole bunch of us kids weren't playing hopscotch or giant steps down near Acadia, Effie and I rode our bicycles around town and talked some more. She was as familiar and as comfortable to me as an old glove.

Still, it would be nice to add Cordelia to my collection

of friends. She could be special without Effie being any less best. And it was clear that Cordelia didn't fit into the category of an old glove.

That afternoon, I told Effie that I had to run an errand for my mother, and left Herbin's jewelry store at two forty-five. I wanted to be alone during my first visit with Cordelia. Later, we could all be together, but not the first time.

When I reached home, I took a look in the icebox. There was a plate of brownies in there that I knew my mother was saving for a small coffee party she was having on the following morning. I removed four of them, wrapped them in waxed paper, and took them to my room. I also carried up a large bottle of ginger ale and two glasses. Then I sat down to wait. It was exactly three o'clock.

She was late. By the time it was three fifteen, I was not quite as confident as I had been, earlier in the day. Maybe she hadn't heard correctly, and was at this instant ringing another doorbell. Maybe her mother hadn't let her go; after all, she hadn't even asked. Maybe she'd changed her mind. Maybe the whole town was just too boring for her.

At three thirty the doorbell rang. I shot downstairs, Charlie, two steps at a time, to answer it. But at the bottom of the stairs I stopped, checked my braids, smoothed my sundress over my stomach, and opened the heavy front door slowly, casually.

"Oh, hello," I said, my voice lazy and nonchalant. "How's the unpacking coming along?"

"Why's your door closed?" she said. "It's hot."

"To keep the heat outside," I said. "It's cool in here. C'mon upstairs. We can have brownies and ginger ale."

For the first half hour she said almost nothing, while I soldiered on, doing most of the talking. I told her about school and our teacher for next year, a real battle-ax of a woman. I also described my friends, Charlie, telling good points about them and a few funny bad points—Grace Maloney's tendency to walk like a duck, for instance, and Matthew Sorensen's twitchy eye. I talked about the dikes, the whales that people saw off Digby Neck, the high tides, the fields full of apple blossoms in the springtime. I mentioned the fun we all had on Saturdays, sitting on the stone wall on Main Street, watching the town come alive with weekend shoppers. I told her some of the things we whispered about these people as they walked up and down on the sidewalk in front of us. I mentioned Mrs. Harrison's enormous stomach in which she kept the baby that was

going to get born *any minute,* and how Mrs. Jackson said
Mrs. Harrison had no business being outside on the street
in that condition. And Avery Harkness's stupid little *red*
goatee and bristly hair, which made him look like a turkey.
Or the way Miss Veronica Hollis kept walking up and
down Main Street each Saturday morning until she had a
chance to say hello to Ambrose Simpson, when everyone
in town knew that he didn't care if she lived or died.

Cordelia Clark sat there, eating three of the four brownies and helping herself to a third glass of ginger ale. She was
thinking. It was easy to see that. For a while, she didn't take
her eyes off me, and I could tell, I was sure I could tell, that
she was very interested in everything that I had to say.
Finally, Cordelia got up and started walking around my
bedroom. Silently, carefully, as I talked on, she looked at
everything—the small china ornaments I'd collected, a
couple of dolls sitting on my bed, flanking a yellow teddy
bear. My books. The drawing (a good one) that I'd left on
the desk so that she'd be sure to notice it. Ribbons for
running, and for jumping higher than anyone else at the last
two Sports Days. A picture of my great-grandmother looking very grand in an old-fashioned lace dress.

Finally, Cordelia swung around and looked at me. Interrupting me in the middle of a sentence, she said, "I've chosen you to be my best friend." Suddenly she was all smiles, unfrozen.

Now *there* was a shock, Charlie, and I didn't know how to deal with it.

"Well," I said, "I do already have a best friend." I paused, and did some fast thinking. "But I'm sure a person can have two. Best friends, that is."

Cordelia's smile faded, but she continued to watch me carefully as I rattled on. "Of course," I said, "I have many"—I emphasized that—"*many* friends, and I bet we can all have a lot of fun together. You're going to be so glad you moved to Wolfville."

"I have to go," she said, gulping down her fourth glass of ginger ale. "Tomorrow's Sunday. I'll be over at two o'clock." And she was gone, down the stairs, across the hall, opening and slamming the big front door. I could hear my mother calling out to me, "Trudy! Where's that last bottle of ginger ale I've been saving for your father?" I pretended not to hear.

Effie and I had planned to walk along the dikes on the following afternoon. But I guessed we could go together, all three of us. Oh, well . . .

♦   ♦   ♦

The three of us did walk together on the dikes, although Cordelia said she didn't know how we could enjoy doing anything so boring. She stuck fast to Effie, letting me walk on ahead, alone.

I stiffened with shock as I heard Cordelia saying to Effie, "See how she's holding her shoulders so straight and her head so high? Does she think she's a queen or something?" And then, "Stuck-up or what?"

Suddenly, for the first time in my life, I didn't know what to do with my body. Normally well-coordinated, I tripped over rocks, slipped and almost fell on a wet patch of grass.

"Poor Trudy," I could hear Cordelia saying, very low. "I feel sorry for anyone that clumsy."

All the way home, Cordelia talked animatedly to Effie, never once addressing a word to me. Their peals of laughter were shrill, their speaking voices barely more than a whisper. What were they saying? What was so funny?

Were they talking about *me?*

But when we parted at Effie's house—when the door closed behind her—Cordelia was her old self—the one I'd caught glimpses of on the previous afternoon.

"I like being your best friend," she said, fixing the ribbon on one of my braids. "I love your long pigtails. I love your white shoes." Then: "I'll be over tonight after we have dinner. At seven thirty."

I was relieved, Charlie, but certainly confused.

Everyone in Wolfville had supper at five thirty, so it was a long wait to seven thirty. However, when she finally turned up, we had fun. She was lively and amusing, with all kinds of ideas about what to play and how to play it. She made the rules, but this was okay with me. As they say nowadays, I could go with the flow. She went on and on about how much she liked being with me. Maybe none of the stuff that had taken place in the afternoon had really meant anything. I enjoyed myself, and agreed to go swimming with her the next day.

"Effie'll come, too," I said.

She sighed, and then grumbled, "Oh, all right."

The next day was blisteringly hot, so I could hardly wait to reach the spot on the river where we'd agreed to meet. The afternoon air was still and heavy—the kind of weather that often precedes a thunderstorm. The dull green leaves, sucked dry by too much sun, hung limp on most of the trees, and no breath of wind stirred them. I could feel the weight of the sun on the top of my head, like a heavy hand, pressing.

Effie and Cordelia were already there. I ran toward

them, jumping lightly over gaps in the rocks, agile as a mountain goat, the heat forgotten. They were shrieking with laughter, and I was eager to join in the fun. But when they saw me, their laughter stopped abruptly, and was replaced by a snicker—from which friend I couldn't tell. There was a long silence as I climbed down the riverbank, stumbling again, awkward.

"Sorry to be late," I said, although I knew I was on time. I felt apologetic, superfluous. And very frightened.

The bushes parted on the other side of the stream, and four figures appeared: Jane Stroth, Julia Sullivan, Grace Maloney, and Matthew Sorensen.

"Hi, kids," I yelled, rising to the occasion, eager to display my intimate acquaintance with Cordelia Clark. "This is the new girl. She's Cordelia. And these are Jane and Julia and Grace and Matthew."

Cordelia stood up and looked at all of them very carefully. Then she turned to Grace and said, "Not Grace Maloney? Not the one that Trudy says walks like a duck? You don't. I noticed. You're very graceful." Then she looked sideways at me, and added, "Unlike some other people I could mention."

It was difficult for me to believe that this was happening. What kind of sheltered life had I been living, Charlie, if I didn't know that cruelty existed? But I learned quickly. I knew then with certainty that before the afternoon was over, mention would be made of my remark about Matthew's twitchy eye. It was just a matter of waiting for it to happen.

That evening, I called Effie on the telephone. "C'mon over," I said. "I've just learned a new card game. We can play it. Or," I added, "just talk."

There was a pause on the other end of the line. "Cordelia asked me over," she said, warily. "I told her I'd go."

What went on in Cordelia's house that evening, Charlie, remains a mystery. I still don't know exactly what she said about me that made Effie so nervous the next time we saw each other.

We were outside Porter's, both of us running errands for our mothers in opposite directions. Our eyes met, and then hers shifted off mine and looked at a spot to the left of my right ear. "Oh," she said. "Hi, Trudy. Nice day."

Effie had never said it was a nice day in her entire life. Besides, it wasn't. It was overcast and deadly hot, and she was a person who detested the heat.

"Have a good time last night?" I asked, my voice careful and light. "Is the house really something special inside?"

There was no way I was going to roll over and let this happen to me without a struggle.

"Yes," said Effie, her eyes roving all over the place, her uneasy feet obviously eager to be gone.

"What's wrong?" I asked.

"Nothing," said Effie. Then she paused. "But she told me some things."

"What things? What are you *talking* about?"

"You know what things. How could you *not* know? I don't want to talk about it."

"*What* things?" I felt frantic. I wanted to take hold of Effie's collar and shake her till her teeth rattled.

"About me. The things you told her about me. Like the stuff you said about Grace and Matthew and about Avery Harkness looking like a turkey. Stuff like that."

"I *never!* I never said anything about you! What did she say I said?"

"She wouldn't tell me," said Effie. "Which I think was very *kind* of her."

Then she was gone, racing down the street toward the drugstore.

I stood on the hot pavement, Charlie, freezing cold in the sweltering heat, hardly breathing. The gigantic Mrs. Harrison lumbered by, but I hardly noticed her size or her rolling gait. I did see Grace Maloney on the other side of the street, eating ice cream with Julia Sullivan. They looked over at me and whispered something behind their hands. Then they laughed, and in the spate of conversation that followed, I could hear one word, "Cordelia," standing out from all the rest.

When I turned a corner and started up to my house, I came face-to-face with her—with Cordelia. I could feel myself recoiling, as though to avoid a physical blow. What would she do this time?

Her face lit up with joy when she met me. I saw it. I knew it was real. But I didn't know what it meant or how to cope with it. Even now, sixty-five years later, it is unclear to me what I could or should have done. When you're eleven years old, and your whole life has suddenly turned inside out, you feel as though you can't handle anything at all. Only two things were clear in my mind: I had to pretend that everything was all right, and I mustn't, under any circumstances, cry.

"Can I come over tonight, after supper?" she said. "And maybe play cards or listen to your father's radio or something?"

"Okay," I said, smiling, my face feeling like stiffening

cement. "But we don't have a radio," I added. I looked at her small animated face, her eager smile, her perky little dress, her white sandals. Suddenly I realized that the dress and the sandals were almost identical to mine. Gone were the New York suit and the pink patent-leather shoes. How had she managed to do that so fast? She had even taken her long, curly hair and forced it into two spindly braids.

"Seven thirty," she said, and turned to go. Then she turned back and grabbed my hand. "I've never had a friend like you," she whispered. "My whole life I've wanted and wanted a perfect friend—all my own and special."

That evening, Cordelia was electric with fun and vitality. After a time, I lost my frozen feeling, and relaxed in her company, laughing as hard as she did, feeling my old self again. We played cards, talked, ate gingersnaps (no more brownies in the icebox), made paper dolls. At nine thirty, my mother came in and shooed her home—nicely. "Time you were off home, Cordelia," she said. "It's almost pitch-dark."

Cordelia turned her large brown eyes upon my mother, and sighed. "Mrs. Hutchinson, I just love having Trudy as my best friend. Everyone loves her, and now she's mine. She's my very own best friend."

"And Effie's, too," said my mother. "It's nice that you can all have such fun together."

A shadow swept Cordelia's smile off her face. Her dancing eyes turned still and sullen. But my mother had already gone back to the living room to join my father.

Later, when I went in to kiss her good night, she looked at me and smiled. "What a lovely girl, Trudy," she said. "She's a real sweetheart."

As I left the room, I could hear her say to my father, "Weird, isn't it, that two such odd parents could produce such a winner? Makes you think."

This split existence went on for six months, Charlie. Week after week, and eventually month after month, I stood by and watched, as she tried to steal everything I did and had and was. I felt as though my personality were being stripped from me in layers, each one coming loose and shriveling on the ground. My jokes—once so spontaneous and funny—landed with a thud. I stopped making them. My posture caved in; glimpsing myself in a store window, I could see that my shoulders sagged, my small stomach stuck out. Fear was with me when I awoke in the morning. It was still there when I lay in bed at night, staring at the dark ceiling.

My mother could see that something was amiss. "Why

do you seem so tired all the time, Trudy? Are you okay? Does anything hurt?"

Yes, in fact, everything hurt—even my body. Joints ached, my head throbbed, my stomach was in a constant knot, my appetite plummeted. But all I said was, "I'm okay. Everything's fine."

My mother was a worrier. If I told her my tale of woe, she'd be so upset that I'd just have something extra to worry about—her. And she might try to interfere. That was a possibility that struck new terror into my heart.

One day, my mother asked, "Where's Effie, these days?"

"Around," I muttered, and retreated to my room.

In the meantime, Cordelia continued to come to my house in order to spread her sunshine and to claim my friendship.

This became almost intolerable for me. How do you smile and smile, when what you really want to do is tear someone limb from limb? During these visits, I became more and more silent, hating the phony part I was playing, detesting the relationship.

Occasionally, very occasionally, we went to her house. Her father sat alone in his huge wood-paneled study, with the door closed.

"What's he studying?" I asked.

"Oh," Cordelia said airily, vaguely, "stuff, I guess."

Her mother came and went, draped in a hundred different dresses, moody and preoccupied, sighing a lot, always looking like a picture out of *Vogue* magazine.

"Gee!" I marveled. "Is she ever pretty!"

"So I'm told," said Cordelia, through her teeth.

She had lots of toys, expensive ones—dolls with real human hair, a huge bear that was as tall as she was, board games, boxed sets of books, her own little Victrola, puzzles, crayons, colored paper—but she preferred to play at my house, particularly when her mother was away. "I don't like to be alone with my father," she said.

"Why?" I asked.

"No reason," she said. "I just don't." Then, "Let's go over to your house. I love it there."

The next day in school, she'd be making fun of the way I played dodgeball, or snickering as a group of my friends— my *friends*—laughed their heads off as I passed by.

At night I prayed with more intensity than I'd ever done in my life. "Please, God, make the Clarks leave town. If someone has to die in order for this to take place, go ahead and let it happen. Make Cordelia nice. Make her stop. Deliver me from evil. Make that family *go, go, go*. Give me back Effie. Give me back my other friends. Make it so that

I never have to see Cordelia Clark again, as long as I live. Please, God. Oh, please, please, *please*. Amen."

But always, the next day, nothing had changed.

One day as Cordelia was prancing around my bedroom, hugging my own small bear, telling jokes, relating tales about her escapades with the girls who had once been my friends, eating my mother's chocolate cookies, praising our friendship, I suddenly heard a voice yelling, a voice remarkably like my own. It screamed, "Get out of here! Go home to your dumb father and your floozy mother, and never set foot in this house again!" I pointed to the door. *"Go!"* I shouted. *"I hate you!"*

I was amazed that my voice could be saying all that—without any directions from me. I never would have had the courage to will myself to say such things. I was both horrified and immeasurably relieved. I knew that it would make Cordelia even more cruel to me, but for that day at least, I didn't care. It was enough for me, Charlie, that I had evicted her from my room, my house. I felt as though I had removed something highly contaminating from my life.

I'm sure you must be wondering, Charlie, what happened next. Telling our sorrows out loud is supposed to be good for us. But the thought of talking about the five months that followed that scene makes my stomach curl up like an overcooked noodle.

However, I can tell you a few things. When school started, our "battle-ax" of a teacher, Mrs. Hector, apprised of my description of her, acted accordingly. So there was not even any refuge for me in the classroom. Cordelia fawned on Mrs. Hector, flattered her, melted her iron heart, ran errands for her, brought her shiny red apples, stayed after school to clean the blackboard and to *talk*. Mrs. Hector disliked me more with each passing day.

After her eviction from my house, Cordelia searched for other best friends, and always she took the same route. Divide and conquer. Destroy and possess. Each girl reacted with surprise and delight when she was chosen. Then I watched Cordelia play her whispering game with every one of them, and witnessed the growing anxiety in their troubled eyes. One by one, she picked them up and dropped them, and from time to time I caught her gazing at me with a grudging longing. No one stood up to her; no one called her bluff. Retaliation was in the wings, ready to pounce. Cordelia sowed fear in her garden of friends.

By the time the Clark family left Wolfville, exactly eleven months and four days after they had arrived, my friends had discovered who Cordelia was. I won't say that they flocked back to me in one thundering horde. They were too embarrassed. They dribbled back, one by one (all except Grace Maloney and Matthew Sorensen), and a couple of them even apologized—never an easy thing to do, Charlie, especially at age eleven, or by that time, twelve.

Nobody in Wolfville knew why the Clarks left, or where they went. Maybe a few men of the town knew (possibly Mrs. Clark passed along information about this during one of her nocturnal visits), but they certainly weren't telling anyone. The three Clarks simply cruised down Main Street and out onto the highway one Thursday afternoon in their black McLaughlin Buick, and almost no one saw them go. They left during school and work hours. If the mayor of Wolfville witnessed this departure from his office window, he didn't rush out to shake their hands and wish them well.

On the following day, four large trucks pulled up to the front door and removed all their belongings—the dolls with the real hair, the giant teddy bear, the piano that no one played, Mr. Clark's heavy study furniture, trunks full—one assumed—of Mrs. Clark's exotic wardrobe. There were no mammoth moving vans in those days, Charlie. They even had to send someone off to Kentville for a fifth truck.

I revised my view of God. He was a little slow in His response to my prayers, but, late or not, He'd actually done it. I took some pride, Charlie, in the fact that I remembered to thank Him.

"I never did say those things about you to Cordelia," I said to Effie, one day, two weeks later.

She was still having difficulty looking me in the eye. We were standing by her backyard gate, and she was drawing circles in the dirt with the toe of her shoe.

"I know," she said. She'd been Cordelia's best friend for a few weeks, and she'd found out what it was like to be possessed by her.

We returned to our friendship, but it was somewhat restrained, and remained so. Never again would we offer each other such juicy confidences, guilty secrets, tainted gossip. For a long time, we were nervous about laughter if it came from the other side of the street, or from a passing car. We saw danger in eyes that didn't meet ours directly, and in those that stared too intently. Years later, when we couldn't even remember exactly what she looked like, we would feel a genuine physical pain (mine in my stomach, Effie's in her head) when her name was mentioned. *Cordelia*—the literary symbol of love.

But I'm okay, Charlie. By and large, I'm okay. After sixty-five years, I suppose this is hardly surprising. But I was very interested in my reaction yesterday to Mr. Zwitz. Because I'm looking at myself very hard these days. This September my school is going to celebrate the sixty-fifth anniversary of our grade six class. Grace Maloney of the duck walk got a postcard last week from Cordelia. She's coming. Cordelia will be here again. And Charlie, I'll admit something to you, but certainly not to anyone else— not even to Effie.

I'm scared.

Big Little Jerome

Jerome Seaboyer was always small. He was born in the village of Periwinkle Pond on the South Shore of Nova Scotia, where his father was a fisherman, and where everybody knew something about everybody else. On his arrival, the other mothers gathered around and clucked, "Oh my, oh my! So little. I hope he's okay." They held their own big, sturdy babies smugly, and looked with pity at his mother.

Mrs. Seaboyer, just home from the hospital with her tiny bundle, felt anger rise in her throat and said coolly, "He's fine. He's perfect. He's beautiful." Secretly she thought the other babies fat and lumpy, but she did not say so. Nor did he admire their eyes or their feet or their gassy smiles.

Instead she said, "I'm beginning to feel a bit tired," and held open the front door. The women left, well satisfied with their visit. But small lines appeared between Mrs. Seaboyer's eyebrows. She sat down on the bottom step of the stairway, and worried. She worried off and on for the rest of her life.

Even when Jerome started to get older, he kept on being small. He walked by himself at nine months, and Mrs. Rhodenizer said it gave her the creeps to see anything that little walking around. Mrs. Seaboyer took note of the fact that Harrison Rhodenizer was fourteen months old and still couldn't do anything but sit. She didn't say so, right out. She smiled sweetly at Mrs. Rhodenizer and asked, "Should I push the sharp things to the back of the table so that Harrison can't hurt himself?" knowing full well that she could have put hand grenades on the table without Harrison's being in any danger at all.

When Jerome was finally old enough to go to school, Mrs. Seaboyer waved good-bye as he boarded the school bus for the first time. She wondered how he could possibly survive at school. He looked young enough to be in diapers, and there he was, leaving her sheltering arms for seven hours every day.

Actually, Mrs. Seaboyer could have relaxed. Jerome did

just fine. At five and a half years old, he was full of fun and always knew how to make people laugh, even on foggy days and during hurricanes. He was very smart, and he sailed through school with high marks and bright ideas. He was a good swimmer and a quick runner, and he won all the track-and-field ribbons for any event requiring speed. The gym instructor named him "Grease" because, he said, he was like greased lightning. But even when Jerome was in fourth grade, people would stop him on the road, stoop down on a level with his nose, and ask, "Do you go to school yet, little boy?" He used to laugh and say, "Sure! I'm in fourth grade!" and then wait to enjoy their looks of surprise. Jerome was a very happy person.

But this state of affairs could not go on forever. Unlike Jerome, Mrs. Seaboyer could look ahead, and maybe that's why those lines never left the center of her forehead. She knew that one day Jerome would wake up and realize that when a man gets older, a lot of things are easier and more pleasant if he's tall. Sure enough, the day after his thirteenth birthday, Jerome met Mrs. Rhodenizer in Dorey's Variety Store. She looked down at him and said, "My heavenly days, Jerome! Still so *small!* For goodness sakes, you'll be in high school next year and all the girls will be taller than you. Aren't you *ever* going to get any bigger?" Jerome felt a cold wind blow across his heart. He didn't know what to say. He looked for a second into her nearsighted eyes; they were peering down at him through glasses so thick they looked like the bottom of pop bottles. He felt like an insect stuck on a pin. Then he lowered his gaze roughly in the direction of her belly button. "Maybe so. Maybe no," he chanted lightly. Mrs. Rhodenizer thought his reply was rude, and said so. Of course, Harrison Rhodenizer was more than five feet six already and his voice was starting to change. He also did poorly in school, fell all over his feet, and was as fat as a pudding.

From that moment on, Jerome became a secret worrier. He realized that what Mrs. Rhodenizer had said was absolutely correct. The girls were taller than he was, including Andrea Doucette, the prettiest girl in his class. Andrea sat in front of him at school, and he loved to look at the back of her head and the way the sun shone on her long, straight, blond hair. Sometimes he would just sit there and think up words to describe it: honey, gold, wheat, sunshine, dandelion.

It is true that Andrea seemed to like Jerome. When she was class president, she always chose him first for spelling bees and relay races. But this was middle school. What about next year? Being short could really begin to matter in high school.

Jerome started locking himself in the bathroom in order to measure his height against the towel rack, and to inspect his face for signs of whiskers. The towel rack stayed in the same place, and so did Jerome. His small handsome face was as smooth as paper. His body was well built and muscular—all four foot six of it. He had thrilling dreams in which he was seven feet tall, his face lost behind a thick, jet-black beard. In these dreams he spent a lot of time saving less gifted swimmers from drowning—people like Harrison Rhodenizer, who couldn't swim a stroke. And night after night he carried Andrea Doucette out of burning buildings, single-handed.

Jerome started to develop lines between *his* eyebrows. Outwardly he was the same as ever: full of jokes, everyone's pal, the life of the party, athletic, smart. But inside, he had sinking feelings. He could visualize a long life ahead of him as an undersized bachelor, reading his books and eating his dinners alone in a pint-sized house, while other men came home to tall, loving wives and enormous families.

Mrs. Seaboyer, who could usually tell exactly what

Jerome was thinking, did all she was able to. She searched for clothes in small sizes that did not seem like kindergarten styles. She fed him masses of vitamins and prayed for growth. She read articles on the mysteries of the pituitary gland. She told him that he looked, and was, marvelous. Jerome admired her strategy, but he saw through it.

His father, for his part, pretended his son was of normal size, and taught him all the fishing lore he knew. Jerome learned about the inshore fisheries, could dress a fish with flair, knew how to recognize the right wood for making lobster traps, and could mend a net and prop up a wharf as well as anybody. He was as prepared for life as it was possible for him to be. But he heard the women whisper when he passed, "A sweet boy! Sad!" And he hated it when the men referred to him as "a nice little feller."

Then his voice changed. It happened gradually, with the usual embarrassing cracks and lurches in his vocal chords. But soon—much sooner than with the other boys—his voice was complete. And it was magnificent. It was deep and rich and powerful. He sang in the bathtub at top volume. He thought up excuses to talk in class. His shouted instructions on the basketball court and at the skating rink were thundering.

But once the first thrill was over, Jerome's vocal talent

threw him further into fits of depression. The contrast between what he was and what he was not was so obvious that he felt more ridiculous than he had before. What was this king-sized voice doing coming from a little boy's body? To add to his problems, things kept coming up at school that worried him. Things like the Christmas dance. Jerome knew he would sit at home and watch TV and wish he were dead. He decided to concoct an illness. Twenty-four-hour stomach flu would do. Certainly no girl would want to dance around the gym with *him*.

One Thursday afternoon, Jerome met Andrea Doucette as he was leaving the variety store. They were talking about homework and the usual things, when suddenly Andrea blurted out, "Jerome, would you like to go to the dance with me?" He was stunned. All he could think to say was, "Oh. Well. Okay. I guess so." Then he turned and left her standing on the steps of the store. In a kind of trance, he walked as far as the breakwater. He stopped then, and stared out at the horizon, full of amazement. Finally he swung around and looked at Andrea. She was staggering under the weight of two bags of groceries, and suddenly they went crashing to the ground. When Jerome rushed back to help, he saw tears in her eyes. Picking up the groceries, he asked, "What's the matter? Why are you crying?"

"I'm not, *really,*" she said, blinking her eyes. "It's just that I'm shy, and you're popular and athletic, and I'm just me. And all you said was, 'Oh. Well. Okay. I guess so.' It was like you slapped me."

Jerome just looked at her. He looked *up* at her, of course, because she was taller than he was. Then he told her he had been too surprised to say anything. As he carried her groceries home for her, he talked about being short, and how awful it was.

Andrea stopped in her tracks and stared at him. "What do you want, Jerome Seaboyer?" she asked, brown eyes flashing. *"Everything?"* Then she looked even fiercer, and went on, "Who do you want to be, if you don't want to be you? Harrison Rhodenizer? Robert MacIntosh? Your father? Ewart Boutilier? Oh, for Pete's sake!"

Suddenly Jerome needed to be alone. He thrust the groceries down on Andrea's porch and muttered, "Gotta go. See you tomorrow." Then he rushed home and picked up his ice skates, and ran all the way to Little Gull Lake.

The lake was smooth and untouched. Most people liked to skate on Morrison's Pond, because it was bigger. But here, there was not a mark on the ice. He put on his skates and went out to the rock that broke the surface in the middle of the lake. There he sat down to think. He was in possession of a certain thought, and he needed enough quiet to look at all sides of it. *Did* he, as Andrea had suggested, want *everything?* Well, yes, as a matter of fact, he did. He knew he had almost all of the things that most people wanted out of life, but he longed for that one special, important, extra thing that would make everything perfect.

Jerome rested his chin on his fist and thought some more. Okay then, did he want to be Harrison Rhodenizer? Poor old, dumb old Harrison Rhodenizer, who had to put up with his nosy mother? No, *thanks*. And Robert MacIntosh? No. He was tall, but he had rotten teeth and his parents drank all the time. His own father, then? A great guy, of course, but *old*. Half of his life was over. He did nothing but work. What about Ewart Boutilier? That was trickier. Andrea must have thrown in that name to make him think. *Really* think. Ewart Boutilier was the tallest boy in the class, handsome, popular, and intelligent. The girls chased after him, or stood around in the halls and giggled when he walked by. He was even *nice*. Jerome thought hard about Ewart. And then, suddenly, he knew. He would like to have *parts* of Ewart—his height, and his fatal charm with the girls. But he did not want to *be* Ewart Boutilier. He, Jerome Seaboyer, wanted to be Jerome Seaboyer. He wanted his own parents, his own special friends, his brains, his sense of humor, his house, his own thoughts and feelings and loves—even his own fears and hates and worries. He wanted to be himself.

Jerome felt as though a ton had been lifted from the back of his neck. He rose from the rock and started to skate, wildly, beautifully, around the lake. He skated in curves and circles, jumping over rocks and spinning around cracks, and then racing at dangerous speeds from one side of the lake to the other. He threw his arms wide, and with his beautiful voice shouted to the trees, "I'm *me*! I'm *me*!" Up above, the sky was blue and cloudless and high. Jerome Seaboyer felt as though he could touch it.

Dreams

I was sixteen years old when he took my dream away from me. It is not a small offense to be a stealer of dreams.

Our family lived in Mackerel Cove, a small fishing village on the South Shore of Nova Scotia. When I tell people that, when I point out the exact location, they look at me with a puzzled, almost incredulous expression. Sometimes that look is all I get. Other times, they give voice to their astonishment. "But how did you become what you are? How did you get from there to here?"

What do they think goes on in small fishing communities? Nothing? Do they assume that such places contain people with no brains, no ambition, no dreams? They look at me as though my skin had just turned green. As though I'd been cast in some inferior mold and had, by some miracle of agility or cussedness, found a way to jump out of it. By the time those questions started, I was a junior executive in an oil company, in the days before oil became a questionable commodity—in Toronto, where the mold is often even more fixed than elsewhere.

When I was a boy of eleven, the horizon was endless, physically and in my mind. From our yellow frame house—which was perched on a hill, without the protection or impediment of trees—you could view the wide sea, stretching from the rocky point and behind Granite Island, disappearing beyond the edge of the sky, inviting dreams of any dimension. And in the foreground, four reefs threw their huge waves up into the air—wild, free.

I spent a lot of time sitting on the woodpile—when I was supposed to be cutting wood, piling wood, or carting wood—looking at that view. And thinking. Planning. Rumor had it that if you drew a straight line from our front door, right through the center of that horizon, the line would eventually end up on the west coast of North Africa. How can Torontonians conclude that such an environment is limiting? They're lucky if they can see through the smog to the end of the block. I could go straight from the woodpile to Africa. Or I could turn left and wind up in Portugal.

And the wind. On that hill, where my great-grandfather had had the vision to build his house, the wind was always a factor. Even when it was not blowing. Then my mother would emerge into the sunshine or the fog, and take a deep breath. "Gone," she would announce. She hated the wind. She was from near Truro, where the slow, muddy Salmon River just limps along its banks, shining brown and slithery in the dead air. Dead air—that's what inlanders seem to want. Then they feel safe. Or peaceful. But those were two words that meant nothing to me at that time.

What is it about kids that makes them so blind and deaf for so long? Some of them, anyway. How can they go charging into life with such a certainty that all is well? Without, in fact, a passing thought as to whether it is or is not? It's just there. Mackerel are for jigging, the sea is for swimming, a boat is for rowing around in. The gulls are for watching, particularly on those days when the wind is up, when they just hang high in the air, motionless, wings wide, riding the storm. I was like that when I was eleven, sailing along with no effort, unconscious of the currents and turbulence that surrounded me.

Twelve seems to be a favorite age for waking up. What is so special about twelve that makes it so hazardous, so brittle? No doubt it's partly because of all those puberty things—those unseen forces that begin to churn up your body, making it vulnerable to dangers that didn't even seem to exist before that time. And with the body, so goes the head and the heart.

All of a sudden (it really did seem to start happening all within the space of a day), I began to hear things. Things like the edge in my mother's voice, the ragged sound of my father's anger. Where had I been before? Too busy on the woodpile, in the boats, at the beach—*outside*. Or when inside, shut off by comic books, TV, the all-absorbing enjoyment of food. And lots of arguing and horsing around with my brothers and sisters, of whom there were five. But now, suddenly, the wind blew, and I heard it.

Once you have heard those sounds, your ears are permanently unplugged, and you cannot stop them up again. Same thing with the eyes. I began to see my mother's face as an objective thing. Not just *my mother,* a warm and blurry concept, but a face to watch and think about and read. It was pinched, dry-looking, with two vertical lines between the brows. Much of the time, I saw, she looked anxious or disenchanted. I didn't know the meaning of that word back then, but I recognized the condition. She was thin and pale of skin—probably because she didn't like to be out in the wind—with a head of defeated-looking thin, brown hair. I saw that for the first time, too.

Within twenty-four hours of my awakening, I felt that I had discovered and recognized everything. My mother, I knew, was worried about money—or about the extreme scarcity of it. That seemed a waste of time to me. There were fish in the sea, vegetables in the garden, loaves of bread in the oven, and secondhand clothes to be had at Frenchy's. But look again. Not just worry. Something else. And that, I knew, had to do with my father. I watched very carefully. He didn't ask for things. He demanded. "Gimme the sugar." "Let the dog out." "Eat your damn vegetables." He didn't praise. He criticized. "This soup is too cold." "There's a rip in them pants." And on pickling day, "Too blasted hot in this kitchen." As he made each one of these remarks, I would see a small contraction in those vertical lines on my mother's forehead. Not much, but to me it was an electric switch. I was aware of a connection.

With this new and unwelcome knowledge, I watched the other kids to assess their reactions. But they were younger than I was. So there was nothing much to watch. They continued to jabber on among themselves, giggling, pushing, yelling at one another. Even when my father would shout, "Shut up, damn you!" they'd all just disperse, regroup, and continue on as before. Well, not quite all. I focused on Amery, age seven, eyes wide and bright, chewing on his nails. Awake, too, I thought, and felt a kinship with him.

My father didn't work as a fisherman in our little village. He was employed in the fish plant, gutting fish. Slash and gut, slash and gut, eight hours a day, five days a week, fifty weeks a year. Enough to limit the vision of any Bay Street Torontonian. I heard people in our village talk about what it was like to work with him. "A real jewel of a man," said one woman to my mother. "Patient, and right considerate. Always ready to help out." I looked at Ma while the woman was talking. I was thirteen by then, and very skillful at reading faces. She's struggling, I concluded, to keep the scorn out of her face. It was a fixed mask, telling nothing— except to me. A man friend of Pa's once said to me, "I sure hope you realize how lucky you are to have a father like him. He's some kind. A real soft-spoken man." I said nothing, and adjusted my own mask. When my father had left the house that morning, he'd yelled back at my mother, "Get your confounded books off the bed before I get home tonight! I'm sick of you with your smart-ass ways!" Then he'd slammed the door so hard that a cup fell off the shelf.

My dream was a simple one. Or so it may seem to you. I wanted to be the most talented fisherman in Mackerel Cove. Talented! I can see the incredulous looks on the faces of my Toronto colleagues and friends. Do they really think that the profession of fishing is just a matter of throwing down a line or a net, and hauling up a fish? A good fisherman knows his gear, his boats, his machinery, the best roots to use when making lobster traps. He knows how to sniff the air and observe the sky for signs of unforecasted winds and fogs. He knows his bait, his times of day, his sea bottom, the choices of where to go and how soon. A talented fisherman knows all these things and much more. And—in spite of the wrenching cold, the disappointments, the fluky comings and goings of the fish population—he loves what he is doing with his life. I know this to be true. I spent half my boyhood tagging along with any local fishermen who'd put up with me—on their Cape Island boats, their Tancooks, or just in their dories.

No one on Bay Street can describe to you the feeling of setting out through a band of sunrise on the water, trailing five seine boats, a faint wind rising. Or the serenity that fills your chest as you strike out to sea, aimed at the dead center of the horizon, focused on Africa. That's what I'd wanted and hoped for from the time I was five years old. At sixteen, it was still my dream.

The exam results came in, just four days before my seventeenth birthday. I stood at the mailbox, holding my marks—the highest in grade twelve for the whole of the county. And more. The biggest university scholarship for that region, puffed out with some fat subsistence money donated by a local boy who'd made good on Wall Street. I took all of it and laid it on the kitchen table.

"I don't want it," is all I said.

My father and mother looked at the marks, read the letter, raised their eyes and looked at me. My mother had her mask on. Not my father.

"What in blazing hell do you mean—you don't *want* it?"

"I don't want to go to college. I want to stay here. I want to be a fisherman. The best one around. It's what I've always wanted, ever since I laid eyes on a boat."

My father stood up. He was skinny, but he looked big that day. With one abrupt gesture, he swept everything off the kitchen table onto the floor—four coffee mugs, the *Daily News,* cutlery, Ma's books, a pot with a geranium in it, a loaded ashtray.

"You want to be a fisherman!" he shouted. "Us with no

gear, no wharf, no shed, no launch. Not even a decent-size boat. No, young fella! You turn down that offer and you got but one route to take. Me, I'll teach you how to do it, because I'm the best gutter in the plant."

He paused for a breath. Then again—"*No,* dammit! You just pitch out your dumb dreams and grab that scholarship, because I'm sure not gonna keep you here any longer, come fall. Not if you can make money with that fool book-learning that your prissy ma seems to have passed along with her mother's milk." He smashed his fist down on the empty table, and kicked his way out the back door.

Ma died when I was twenty-four, just one week before I received my M.B.A. from the University of Toronto. I'd picked up two other degrees on the way, and had sailed through college with accolades and scholarships. There I was, half an orphan, embarking on a life of prosperity and maladjustment, cut off by my past and my present from my original dream.

I skipped graduation and flew home for the funeral. I stayed three weeks. Pa was silent and shrunken-looking, although he was only fifty-five. He sat around a lot, guzzling beer, going through two packs of cigarettes a day. The only kid left at home was Amery, and he looked as though he'd like nothing better than to jump ship. Thin and fidgety, he'd startle if you so much as snapped your fingers. He was working in the plant, too. Gutting.

"Thinkin' o' closin' down the plant," said Pa, one day. "No fish worth a darn. Most o' the time, anyways. Foreign vessels scoopin' 'em all up before they has a chance to spawn."

He didn't say this angrily. He said it wearily, as though he had nothing but lukewarm water flowing through his veins. And no blood transfusion in sight.

The day I left, I waited until Amery and Pa had departed for work. Then I went out and sat on the woodpile. The offshore wind was blowing strong and dry, and the gulls were coasting around in the sky, wings spread, barely twitching. The sun was well up, casting a wide path over the ruffled water. While I watched, a Cape Islander crossed the path, low in the water, with a big catch of mackerel. In the distance, the horizon stretched taut and firm, broken by the leaping waves of the four reefs.

I searched in vain for Africa. It didn't seem to be there anymore.

Was It Fun on The Beach Today?

She had come down to the beach earlier than usual that morning. The air was clear, the shapes sharp and vivid against a cloudless sky, the sun's light still low and golden. An offshore wind blew steadily across the sand and out toward the dancing reefs. Standing up, facing the water, she could feel the cool air whipping her hair forward, as the breeze reached her from above the dunes. Shivering, she dumped her beach gear in an untidy heap on the ground, and lay down beside it on the bare sand. Digging with her fists, she made two shallow depressions for her breasts, and wiggled into them. *There. It's warm down here. The wind can't get at me. Nothing can get at me. Not even Mother.* She pulled her swimsuit—emerald green, tight—over her hips, and brushed her brown hair away from her face. Catlike, she writhed on the sand and pressed herself into its warmth. *I'll have sand in my suit, sand in my hair. She'll say, "Don't track all that sand in over my clean floors." She won't even stop instructing me long enough to ask if it was fun on the beach today.*

"Hi, Julie." Mr. Desmond, the local beachcomber. Retired and bald, with skin like crinkle cotton. Bored and boring.

Julie sat up and hugged her knees.

"Hi, Mr. Desmond. Nice day."

"How come you're down so early? Your gang doesn't usually start cluttering up the beach 'till about ten thirty."

"Cluttering?"

"Oh, you know. Frisbees and what you choose to call music. Splashing and shrieking."

You've forgotten how to be young, Mr. Desmond, darling. She wished she could say it out loud. What satisfaction, what rich revenge.

"We're happy," she said.

He sighed. "Well, enjoy it while you can."

"Thank you," she said tartly. "We will."

He turned to go. "Your bathing dress is very pretty." It was clear from the turn of his head—away from her—that he felt uneasy about his compliment.

Bathing dress. Out of the Dark Ages. She untangled her pile of beach paraphernalia and arranged the items on the sand. King-sized towel with a huge Garfield, winking at her. She grinned, and ran her hand over his terry fur. Can of Coke. Sunscreen lotion from her mother, for protection. Baby oil, for a seductive shine. She moved her watch strap and admired the band of white skin, declaring the depth of her tan. A book of short stories, summer reading for next year's grade nine English class, unopened. A *People* magazine, wrinkled and worn. A pair of mirror sunglasses. *If I'm a spy in the next war, I'll wear sunglasses exactly like these. When they interrogate me* (in her head, she said this word carefully, drawing out the four syllables) *I will stare at them with my two blank eyes, and they will be unnerved by my inscrutability.* She pronounced this last word slowly, too—this time aloud:

"In–scru–ta–bil–i–ty."

"Talking to yourself. Aha!"

She jerked around, startled. "Alicia! You could cough or something, to give a person a warning. You scared me right out of my skin."

"Why ya down so early?"

Julie stared up at Alicia through her sunglasses. *None of your business.*

"Because."

"Because why?"

Alicia thumped her heavy body down on the sand. Double chins. Five pimples. Julie counted them. Stomach.

"Because I wanted to be alone." *Did you hear that, Alicia?*

"Me too. Thank heavens for the refuge of sand and ocean for the comfort of the ravaged soul."

Julie looked at Alicia sideways. Not enough to have a bizarre name and a fat form. At fourteen, it's unappetizing to go around talking about ravaged souls.

"What in particular," asked Julie, spreading baby oil gently, languidly, over her smooth brown legs, "is ravaging your soul this morning?"

"Mother. She can't stop nagging. Or apparently she can't."

"You happen to be defining motherhood," said Julie, putting the top back on the bottle and arranging her towel on the sand. "About what?"

"Three guesses. *Fat.* 'Go easy on the cookies, dear.' 'Why not try jogging this summer?' 'You'd *feel* better, darling, if you lost weight.' 'Out of the ice cream, Alicia.' 'When I was your age, sweetheart, I was a real featherweight.' Can you imagine such torture?"

"Yes."

"Huh. I bet your mom never nags *you.*"

"Don't be dumb, Alicia. If mothers didn't have anything to nag their kids about, they'd invent stuff." Pause. "Fathers are better."

"Sometimes," mumbled Alicia, bleakly.

The girls lay on their stomachs side by side. Julie glanced at Alicia.

"Him, too?"

"Worse." Alicia sighed. "Wants me to *help* all the time. Says I'm *irresponsible. Lazy,* even. Also loves to elaborate on the theme of fat—just like Mom. 'Run to the store for me, Alicia. The exercise will do you good. Maybe take off some of that tummy. *Run,* Alicia!' "

Julie frowned into the sand. But Alicia's parents were right. Alicia looked like . . . what? A whale. Blubbery, rubbery. With a lovely face. Minus zits and with fewer chins, she'd be prettier than Julie. A *lot* prettier.

"Maybe they just want to help."

Alicia snorted. Then, "What on earth can your mother find to nag *you* about?" She looked with distaste at Julie's body. Not one spare pinch of fat, and all the curves in the correct locations.

Julie took a deep breath. "Oh, things." She drew hearts in the sand with her forefinger. "Like my jeans being too tight.

Like too much eye makeup. Like do I have to play my music so loud. Like getting good *grades* so I'll have an affluent and fulfilling *future*. My *future*, for Pete's sake. I'm fourteen years old. My future's in the future, I say. *Now* is where I happen to be on the seventeenth of July. Besides . . ." Julie frowned again.

"Besides what?" muttered Alicia into her arms.

"Besides," Julie cleared her throat, "the future probably won't even happen."

Alicia raised her head and stared at Julie. She watched her in silence for a few moments. Four gulls were gabbling and squawking at the far end of the beach. The waves were going slap, retreat, slap, retreat, and the sea was icy blue.

"What're you *talking* about? You got some awful disease or something? Like cancer or AIDS, or *what*?" Alicia moved just a bit farther away.

"No, dopey." *Dumb.* "I mean about the world killing itself. Dead air. Dead forests. Dead rivers. The bomb and things." Julie sighed. "Why knock yourself out doing algebra and geometry, and learning irregular verbs, and memorizing history dates, and preparing yourself for a future that's not even going to be *there?*"

"Oh c'mon, Julie. It's gonna be *there.*"

"Huh!" Julie slithered over onto her back and felt the sun's warmth on her face. "Better we should be learning six ways to cook dandelion greens."

"What?"

"Oh, forget it, Alicia. Enjoy the sun." *So much for being alone.*

"Julie!" Stage whisper from The Whale.

"What?"

"Brace yourself." Alicia paused. "I can see the slow approach of Richard Hetherington."

Julie flipped over, so that no one would notice her heart beating in her throat.

"So?"

"So the day has begun. The sun has risen. The beach has blossomed. Flowers are growing in the barren sand."

Julie said nothing. She visualized his arrival. *Eighteen years old.* Shoulders like that Greek statue in the history text. Skinny hips. Long hairy legs. *Voice.* Deep, deep voice, soft and caressing. *I want to touch Richard Hetherington.* She moved against the warm sand and waited.

"Hi." Like a Hammond organ.

"Oh," said Julie, raising herself ever so slowly, ever so casually, on one elbow. "Oh," she repeated, "so it's you, Richard. Pull up a towel. Have a piece of sand. Enjoy."

There. I did that very well indeed. Calm and articulate. She settled down once more upon her arms, face hidden.

"Nice suit," said Richard from somewhere above her.

"What?" This from Alicia.

"Julie's suit," said Richard. "Nice."

"You and Mr. Desmond," sighed Julie. "Two of a kind."

"Meaning?"

Julie looked up. Richard was a giant, his head touching the sky.

"Don't ask," Julie said, and pressed her face once more onto Garfield's flanks.

"Great day, eh?" offered Alicia.

"What?" Richard frowned, rubbing his ear, as though searching for a trapped insect. "Oh, yeah. Yeah, great." He spread his towel beside Julie and lay down close to her, his arm a scant finger-width away. Then their shoulders touched, and he turned to her. "Hi, princess." He grinned.

Julie moved her head and pretended to watch the flight of two cormorants close to the surface of the water. With the change of wind and tide, the surf was higher. The green underbelly of water crested, and fell pounding to the sand. Slithering back into itself, the water peaked again and thundered down once more. Julie's breath was coming quickly, as though she were winded from a long run. *Please don't let him hear me breathing. Let me be cool. Let me be in control of this thing.* His finger was moving softly, softly, against her wrist. *If there is a heaven, I am already there.* Then the finger was suddenly still.

Covertly she watched as Richard rose on his elbows and gazed down the beach. His light blue irises, circled by dark rims—like Mel Gibson's—scanned the scene, and suddenly riveted on something.

Then: "I'll give you a report," he said, voice rumbling. There was a pause. "The Body approaches," he went on, "in company with two familiar fillies. Trailing behind this small parade are three lovestruck gentlemen, all of our acquaintance."

Julie's head rose carefully, painfully. Alicia was already focused on the group.

"The Body . . ." began Julie uncertainly.

Richard interrupted, "I think one may assume that The Body belongs to Sylvia's cousin from Boston. An American Body, in short. On a month-long visit, I am told—if one may dare to believe such a miracle of good fortune. I rise," he announced, unfolding himself in one slow, sure movement, "to offer an official Canadian welcome." He sauntered, long-legged and lithe, toward the group. Julie turned to Alicia, suddenly become a dear and comforting ally.

"Well dammit all anyway," she said to Alicia, who replied, "Yes."

The Body was indeed someone to welcome on behalf of any nation. Ash-blond hair tossed in the wind, a creamy tan, tall and oppressively graceful. A slick Siamese among kittens and tabby cats.

"There goes my summer," said Julie.

"I'm going on a diet," groaned Alicia. "This afternoon. This morning. Yesterday. At least he called you 'princess.' "

"That was *before*," said Julie.

"Don't complain. All he said to me was, 'What?' Y'got to admit that 'Hi, princess' is an improvement on *that*."

Within minutes, the air was filled with music from Ted's boom box. Jim was dancing with Sylvia, and Richard Hetherington was chasing The Body into the icy cold water. Mr. Desmond passed by, frowning. Julie and Alicia laughed a lot, danced, duck-dived through the waves, applied baby oil to skin that was already slippery as butter, exchanged agonized glances.

◆　　◆　　◆

"I suppose," said Julie to Alicia as they parted at Julie's cottage at noon, "that I really shouldn't mind this so much. After all, beside him, I'm only a two-bit kid. It's just that it seemed kind of close. I could feel him *scanning* me. He *touched* me, Alicia."

"Well," sighed Alicia, panting from her walk up the hill, "he sure didn't scan *me*. Or touch me. He'd probably *recoil* if he touched me." She fiddled with the strap on her beach bag. "Lookit, Julie, this is the way I figure about guys like Richard."

"What? What do you figure?"

"I figure they're for decoration. For livening up the beach. For nighttime daydreams. He's supposed to be real hot material. Julie?" She paused.

"Yeah?"

Alicia bit her lip. "I don't think you're ready."

"Well, I sure *feel* ready."

"Yeah, well, you're *not*."

"Well . . . *maybe*. Maybe not for the really heavy maneuvers."

"So let's leave him to The Body, and just try to enjoy the performance."

Julie surveyed The Whale. Probably you could afford to be philosophical when you were without hope of any kind.

"I suppose in the future . . ." She paused.

"What future?" Alicia grinned, and her pretty face was bright with amusement. "I thought there wasn't going to be any future."

Julie laughed. "Well," she said, "there's always two ways of looking at everything. 'Bye now. See you this afternoon. Come by on your way to the beach."

She ran down the path to the stairway of her veranda, where her mother was sweeping the steps.

"Hi, Mom!" she said, and gave her mother a swift kiss on the cheek. "Love ya."

"Me too," said her mother. "Don't track all that sand in over my clean floors." Lightly, she touched the side of Julie's face. "Was it fun on the beach today?" she asked.

Janetta's Confinement

She was seven and a half years old, and tall for her age. Her hair was no-color beige, and it hung down, lank and straight, from two hot-pink bunny barrettes. Her face was not striking in either its beauty or its ugliness. No one, in fact, could have predicted how its features would eventually arrange themselves. Puberty was still far off; she had a straight-up-and-down body, legs like posts, long, formless fingers.

Her name was Janetta—apparently the only remarkable thing about her. Sometimes she would write her name on a piece of paper, wait until the ink dried, and then run her index finger across it, stroking, stroking. Other times, she would lock the bathroom door and study herself in the mirror—this way, that way, over her shoulder, straight on. She could make nothing of that face. She came to no conclusions. Then, three weeks might pass before she would look at herself again—*really* look, that is. She would examine her face to make sure that bubble gum wasn't sticking to her chin, or in order to pick her teeth after eating corn on the cob, but that was mainly because her teeth felt tight and uncomfortable. And to check if her barrettes were aligned.

Once she had seen Judy Merino downtown in Scotia Square. Judy was from school, in grade three. She was looking at a display of neon T-shirts—fiery pink, blazing mauve, electric blue, glaring yellow. She was holding them up under her chin, one color at a time, in front of the mirror, taking a long, careful moment to study the effect of each one. On her hair, one purple barrette was firmly fastened beside the upper-right-hand corner of her forehead. The other was dangling from a lock of hair, level with her left earlobe. To the onlooker, her barrettes stood, in fact, at twenty after eleven, or possibly five minutes to four. Janetta was amazed. How could Judy be staring at herself in the mirror *so hard* and yet fail to see those unbalanced barrettes? From then on, before she left for school, Janetta always checked. Every time.

Janetta had once been a baby. This was an astonishing fact for Janetta to absorb. It was too far away; it was beyond memory. But of course, it was true. Everyone starts out as a baby. You don't have to be very old to know *that*. Besides, there were pictures to prove it—snapshots of her grinning through the bars of her crib; looking up at her mother's adoring face; taking her first step (Mom and Dad squatting down in front of her, arms flung out to rescue her from falling); sitting in the bathtub; laughing with her mouth wide open, no teeth in sight. She certainly looked as though she had the world by the tail. Same with the later pictures—blowing out her birthday-cake candles, face ready to burst, age four; swinging in the old tire, legs high in the air, age five; on Bayswater Beach, lying flat on her stomach in the wake of a spent wave, age six; eating cotton candy at the fair, eyes wide, her mouth lost behind a pink beard, age seven.

Best of all Janetta liked the one in which her mother was looking adoringly at her. She was cradling her in her arms (age five months? Who can tell?) and gazing down at her. Her mother was very young and pretty, and in her eyes was such an aching expression of love that when Janetta looked at it, she could feel her eyes stinging at the corners. She also liked the cotton candy picture, but she didn't know exactly

why. Maybe because of the day, which Janetta could remember so clearly. Her father took the picture (and another blurry one of her on the merry-go-round), and no
one else was there. It was like a miracle to have him all to
herself. Mom was at home, throwing up.

That was the start. She threw up a lot, and not just in the
morning. Often she lay down in a curled-up ball, facing the
wall, not even looking at anybody. That lying-down thing
seemed to go on forever and ever. Janetta would watch her
from the doorway, wanting to go in, not daring to. Her
mother seemed like a whole new person. Janetta didn't
know what the ground rules were anymore.

Her father told her, "Mom's feeling pretty awful. Try
not to bother her too much."

Once she said to her mother, "Could we go down to
Point Pleasant Park and look for some ducks to feed?"

Her mother's eyes were sad and unfocused. "I'm sorry,
sweetie," she said, and gave her hand a squeeze. "Not
today. I feel too terrible." She shut her eyes. "I just feel like
I'm dying." Then she got up very quickly and went off to
the bathroom to be sick again.

Dying! Janetta watched the closed bathroom door and
willed it to open. Then her mother came out and lay down
again on the sofa, very pale. "Be patient," she said, her

voice very low and hoarse. "This is only supposed to go on for three months. Then we'll go to the park. We'll do all sorts of wonderful things. Just wait. You'll see." She reached out her arm and gave Janetta a limp hug.

Three months. Another forever. Could you get over dying in three months? But it wasn't three months. It was five. "Just wait," she'd said. Janetta often felt like crying, but she couldn't. If she upset her mother, maybe she wouldn't just *feel* like dying. She could hear her father saying, "Try not to bother her too much." And she couldn't bother *him*. He seemed to be away most of the time.

Then Janetta's mom got bigger and bigger, until Janetta could hardly believe that anyone could be that huge without bursting. She knew, of course, that there was a baby in there—two babies, in fact—but she would have believed it if someone had told her that there were actually four. No wonder her mother was tired. What must it be like lugging around that great big body every single day?

A couple of times, Janetta said to her mother, "Are you ready to go to the park yet?" But her mother sat down and looked at her very hard, reaching out her hand to touch Janetta's cheek.

"Honey," she said, "Daddy's got the car. I'd never make it down there on my own two feet. I feel like a Mack truck. Without wheels. I know it's really hard for you to understand, but I'm just so *weary*. And my back hurts a whole lot. Maybe next week. Right now I feel three-quarters dead."

But next week it was the same. And when Daddy was home, he stuck so close to her mother that it was like he was scared she'd break if he left her alone for two seconds. Break or *die*.

Once Janetta's dad took her to the park, but it wasn't really any fun. He forgot the bread for the ducks, and he was so serious and silent all the time they were gone that she didn't know whether she should talk or not. Almost the only thing he said was, "Babies can come early, you know. And that can be bad." Bad? Why bad? It sounded good to Janetta. Let's get the whole thing over with as fast as possible. But . . . bad. In what *way* bad? She wanted to leave the ducks and go home. She looked at them—mallards, mergansers—but she wasn't really *watching*. They weren't reaching her. She didn't even notice the blue sea and the big ships sliding by so silently. Usually she loved them. Their hugeness made her breath catch. But today she couldn't have told you what shape they were or what color, although she seemed to be staring at them the whole time. But the pictures in her head were stronger, more vivid.

"Let's go home," she said to her dad. "Let's check up on Mom."

"Good idea," he said, taking her hand.

They walked past the container port, and she didn't even stop to marvel at the giant cranes lifting their humongous boxes. They creaked and groaned and slid along their tracks. She didn't look.

Eventually, in mid-August, Janetta's mother went off to the hospital, face tight, hand clutching her back, in Mrs. Simes's car. Mrs. Simes lived next door. It was Monday, and Janetta's father was away. He was a salesman, and during that two-week period he was doing what he always called his "swing around New Brunswick." His boss didn't think that having twins was a good reason to stay home. There were all those orders. In a recession, you can't ignore orders. No siree.

The twins' delivery was complicated, and Janetta's mom had to stay in the hospital for seven days. During that time, Janetta lived at the Nicholsons' house. Mom's last words had been, "Now, be a good girl at the Nicholsons'. It's so kind of them to invite you. She's got four kids of her own. But that should make it fun for you." Then, just before she disappeared into the car, she called back, "Don't forget to say thank you before you leave."

Four kids. Didn't she know it. The baby was really little and seemed to cry most of the time. Even when he was asleep, he made sad whimpering noises. He didn't look one bit like Janetta's happy baby pictures. Then came Lucy, who was four. On the second day, she stood beside Janetta and watched her drawing a very beautiful picture (of her own house and tulip garden, with bluebirds flying in the sky and kittens playing), which she was planning to give to her mother as a welcome-home present. Lucy took one of her crayons and made four big red scribbles across the page before Janetta even realized what was happening. She clenched her hands together to keep them from punching Lucy in the stomach. Then she went up and shut herself in their messy bathroom (towels just tossed over the racks or dumped on the floor, brown rings in the bathtub, tooth-paste tubes left open and dribbling white guck over the sink, not like home), and put her forehead down on the rim of the sink. She'd like to have cried, but she couldn't.

She was trying so hard to be grateful and nice that she felt stiff and tight all over. Holding all that hate inside her was seizing her right up.

Oscar Nicholson was eleven—really old. He kept a dead mouse in his pocket. When his mother was too busy to know what was going on—which was most of the time— he would often pull out the mouse and wiggle it in front of Janetta, close to her face. She thought she might faint from the terror she felt. She didn't know what she was frightened of, but the fear was terrible. Her mouth was dry and she could feel a small thin scream locked in her throat, straining to get out. And when he wasn't scaring her with the mouse, she kept being afraid that he would. She had to keep watching his pocket and what his hands were doing.

But Stella was the worst. Stella was seven and a half years old—the same age as Janetta. She waited until no one else was around, and then she did or said things. On the third day, she said, "Want to play with my doll?" and held it out to Janetta, smiling. Janetta felt she needed badly to have something to hug, and reached out for it hungrily. The instant before her hands touched the doll, Stella snatched it away. "Changed my mind," she snapped, still smiling, but with her lips pressed together and ugly.

One day when they were outside playing in the drizzle,

with the foghorns moaning and lamenting down by the harbor (the weather was awful, all that week), Stella said, "Sometimes people die having babies." Another time she said, "I bet your dad won't come home again, ever. Fathers don't like having too many kids around. *Everyone* knows *that*." Or just, "It must be gross to have straight hair." Stella's was curly and glossy black.

Mr. Nicholson was either silent or crabby. It just depended. "Shut up, you kids!" he'd yell, when the noise got too wild. Mrs. Nicholson was busy. Not for one second did she stop being busy. She walked the floor with the screaming baby, looking frantic, her hair uncurled and fine, hanging in pale strings over her ears, not very clean. She served potato soup or hamburger hash or corned beef and cabbage, so there'd be only one pot to wash. She left the dirty dishes on the counter, piling up and spilling over onto the stove and the sink until there was hardly a spot on which to lay down one small teaspoon. When there were no more dishes left to use, she washed them, usually after everyone else had gone to bed for the night. Janetta listened to her down there, clattering around. Later, she could hear thunking noises in Mr. and Mrs. Nicholson's bedroom. It was hard to sleep.

During that week it often poured with rain, and the

Nicholsons didn't have a dryer. Damp laundry hung from lines strung across the kitchen, sometimes even in the living room and in the back and front porches. When Stella asked her mother something like "Can you look at a picture I drew this morning?" Mrs. Nicholson would say, "Later," or "Not now. I'm too busy," or "Can't you hear the baby crying?" Everywhere you looked, toys littered the floors—torn books, blocks, rattles, naked dolls, balls to trip over. Lucy poked the sleeping baby and the screams began anew. Oscar slapped Lucy, who went and threw Stella's new dinosaur down the dirty cellar steps. Stella dragged Janetta outside on the veranda and told her that twins were often born with no feet. Mrs. Nicholson hung up yet another wash on the crowded lines, face blank.

On Saturday Mr. Nicholson sat in the living room and watched game shows and baseball on TV, clicking back and forth on the remote, biting his nails. Once, when he tripped on one of Lucy's pull-toys, he kicked it so hard that the wheels fell off and went spinning away in all directions. Stella would come up to him and touch his hand, resting on the arm of his chair, and maybe beg, "Can we play cards?" "I'm tired," he'd say. "Don't forget it's me that makes the money around here to keep all your stomachs full of food. I'd like some peace and quiet on the weekends." Then he'd change channels and drown out her complaints with noisy commercials. Sometimes he'd call out, "When's supper?"

At night Janetta lay wide awake, with Stella beside her on the same bed. She was afraid to move, in case Stella woke up and started to tell her more scary things, breathing her nasty night breath over her as she talked. She thought about big families, and how she was soon going to be part of one. She already knew that she had twin brothers, and that they weighed six and a quarter and six and a half pounds, and that they had curly hair. She thought about the twins' feet. She heard snores and snuffling coming from the other rooms. She believed that her father would come home, but she didn't know this for absolute sure. She remembered the day at the fair, and the cotton candy. She could taste the sweetness of it, and the wispy weightlessness. She knew that her mother hadn't died yet, but maybe that happened later, after babies were out of their mothers, and older. She wanted to cry, but she couldn't. Crying can be noisy, and Stella might wake up. Better to clamp her teeth together and hold her breath until the feeling passed.

On Monday of the next week, Mrs. Nicholson spoke to Janetta as she was pushing her cornflakes around the bowl.

"Your mother's coming home today," she said. "Mrs. Simes is bringing her back at ten thirty. Better get your stuff ready. Your pajamas and all. Mrs. Simes'll phone for you when they get there." Why Mrs. Simes? Why not her mother? Never mind. If her mother was coming home, she must be alive, but maybe too far gone to use the telephone. Sick or something. But not dead.

Mrs. Nicholson continued, "When you're ready, go on outside and play with Stella until it's time to leave."

But Stella didn't wait. She grabbed Janetta's hand—too tight, as usual. She pulled her outside and shoved her onto the huge back-porch swing, pushing the floor until it started to move, higher and higher, back and forth.

"Mothers like boys better than girls," she shouted above the squeaky mechanism.

"They don't, either," Janetta said, very low.

But Stella heard her. "Do, too," she hollered. "I got brothers. I *know*. My mom likes them way best. Besides . . ."

"Besides what?" Janetta was yelling now, too.

"When you're almost eight, you're not cute anymore. That's what parents really like. They want their kids to be little and cute and cuddly."

Janetta looked down at her dumpy legs. She felt very

tired. "I gotta go in and pack," she said. She checked the time on her Mickey Mouse watch, her father's present for her seventh birthday. "It's almost ten."

"Stupid-looking baby watch," Stella said, and jumped off, leaving Janetta to clatter back and forth on the massive metal swing until it finally stopped. "Hurry up, slowpoke!" she shouted from inside the house.

Janetta went up the stairs one step at a time, feet heavy. She packed her things into her plastic grocery bag—her pajamas and slippers, her extra underpants, her toothbrush, her stuffed bear. The bear had a black ear now, from the day Lucy attacked him with a black crayon. (Lucy almost never went anywhere without her crayons.) Janetta took the bag and went into the bathroom, locking the door behind her. Maybe she could cry, now. If she did, perhaps that squeezed feeling in her chest would go away. But she couldn't. Stella was outside, pounding on the door, and yelling, "Gotta go! Gotta go! I'm gonna wet my pants!" Janetta opened the door and walked out. When she was able to get back in, the crying feeling was gone.

At 10:30 sharp, the phone rang. Janetta, normally slow moving, shot forward to answer it. The voice at the other end said, "Please tell Janetta she can come home now and see her new brothers."

"I'm Janetta," she said, but Mrs. Simes had already hung up.

Janetta flew out the door. The grocery bag flapped against her legs as she raced down the street. Her house was only two blocks away, but at the end of the first block she suddenly stopped. She stood there for a moment or two, perfectly still, and then she turned around and ran all the way back to the Nicholsons'. She dashed in the front door without knocking. The baby was in his carriage, crying; Lucy was watching cartoons on TV, with the sound turned up to full volume, peeling the paper off a red crayon; Stella and Oscar were fighting over a game of Monopoly, throwing around houses and hotels. Janetta found Mrs. Nicholson out by the washing machine, stuffing dirty laundry into the top.

"Thank you very much," Janetta panted, "for the lovely time."

Then she was gone. In three minutes she was home. At the bottom of the steps she stopped to catch her breath. Boys better than girls. No feet. Too many kids around. Won't come home again, ever. Sometimes die. Cute and cuddly. Straight hair. Slowly she walked up the stairs. She stopped again at the top, and took another deep breath. Then she reached out her hand and opened up her own front door.

Joanna and the Dark

At fourteen, I was very holy indeed, and I knew it. I had not yet heard of the First and Primary Deadly Sin, so I felt free to bask, to wallow, in my own piety. Sitting in church, my hands clasped tightly in my lap, I passed judgment upon those whose halos had long ago slipped from their bald heads, their flowered hats. They were whispering; their minds were not on sacred matters. No one who had a cluster of vermilion cherries on her hat could possibly care about God. The woman who had brought in that snuffling baby should be evicted from the church; God would not want either adenoids or sinuses to interfere with pious thoughts. For the fat man who kept yawning during the sermon, I felt a strenuous, undisguised revulsion.

Fourteen is a time of reckoning or panic for many, but not for me. I knew who I was and why I was sitting in that particular pew. I was Joanna McKelvey, and I was stationed in the back seat of the church because—wishing to be alone with my spiritual intensity—I had chosen to remove myself from my family.

This isolation had been surprisingly easy to accomplish. I had embraced lateness as my ally, and when my father and mother and brothers—Robert and Roger—were ready to leave, I was still sitting on the edge of the bathtub, door locked, water tap in full flood. "I'm not quite ready," I'd called out, smoothing my Sunday dress over my knees. "Go on without me. I'll slip in at the back."

And what bliss it was to be there alone, where I could savor the taste of Good Friday without my mother's nervous fidgeting, freed from Robert's whispers and Roger's chronic cough, removed from the weekly view of Mr. Hickley's shiny pink head with its scattering of white bristles. Here in the last pew, I could see the whole wide center aisle leading up to the chancel and the enormous stained glass window, where Jesus was very appropriately pictured upon the cross. There He was, dying for our sins, of which this church was certainly full, but of which I was mercifully empty. Me and Dr. Fraser.

I had not always been holy. In fact, with a mixture of shame and tolerant amusement born of the weight of my fourteen years, I was aware that as a young child I had hated Sunday school and Sundays. Sunday school was a cold bleak hall with a tinny piano and an ardent supervisor, beating time to the hymns with a chopped-off blackboard pointer. We sang,

> *God sees the little sparrow fall;*
> *It meets His tender view.*

I did not marvel at God's ability to see the fall of each sparrow, nor did I care about it. Besides, as far as I could see, sparrows were all equipped with wings, and did precious little falling. This was dull stuff, and the prospect of the rest of the day was usually no better. With flawed consistency, my father—mild in his attitude toward most things, but rigid about Sundays—permitted swimming and walking and singing on the Sabbath, but sternly forbade skiing, skating, and card games. This meant that summer Sundays were tolerable, and winter ones were not.

One day, tiring of the chilly hall and the dragging hymns, I begged to be allowed to go to church instead of to Sunday school. I would be quiet, I promised. I would be as still and as attentive as the big kids—the twelve-year-olds and up, who were free to come to church because senior Sunday school took place in the afternoon. Yes, I could go, just this once.

Five years later, I could remember that first experience of church as vividly as though it had been the day before. It had been warm, for one thing. I had taken off my heavy winter coat and sat quietly in my navy taffeta dress with its stand-up collar. My hair—not only blond but also curly—tumbled over my head like Shirley Temple's of long ago. "Cute!" I could hear people whisper. "Sweet!"

I smiled quietly, feeling peace and contentment enclose and caress me. The organ music was large and swelling. It filled the aisles, pressed south and north against the rows of colored windows, pushed upward to the very top of the huge vaulted ceiling. The chandeliers sparkled in the induced dimness, and the brilliance of the central window assaulted my eyes, with its sorrowing Christ, its host of followers, doves, lambs, harps, flowers. I felt my small chest poised to explode with a hugeness of sentiment, with the struggle to contain such beauty of sight and sound. The arrival of the minister completed my bliss. With the appearance of an angel (male—as all angels were then thought to be—chiseled and firm of face, tall and powerful of form and self), the Reverend Mr. Gordon Fraser looked down

upon his flock from his raised pulpit, and spoke, in a voice
like another organ in its lower registers.

"Let us pray," he said.

I bent my head, in accordance with my promise of good
behavior, but my eyes were raised and fixed upon that
amazing man. When the time came for him to preach his
sermon, I could watch him less covertly. His gestures had
a dramatic pattern to them that matched his eloquent
speech. When he said "down," his fist descended on the
exact word. When he spoke of expansiveness or hope, his
arms opened wide, on the corresponding beat of the
phrase. The rhythm of his speech and of his body moved
along unerringly in unison. His sermons, his prayers, and
later on his conversations, were a kind of dance. When his
wonderful voice called us all to the good life, to regular
church attendance, to a lifelong devotion to God, I was his
instant follower, his ready-made disciple at the age of nine.
I would have followed him gladly into the pit of hell. To
march behind him into heaven—a Christian soldier—re-
quired no decision. I was already on the move.

Our church was a large one, with a teeming and prosperous congregation. It was situated on an extravagant plot
of land in the midst of rich homes and bright gardens. Far
to the south and west were the traffic and dirt of the

downtown, the noise and evils of the urban marketplace. But there was no noise, no dirt, in this section of the city. To be the minister of Sunnybrook Gardens United Church was to be in a position of prestige, wealth, power. I was therefore in no danger of losing Mr. Fraser. No other church would be likely to snap him up, offering a larger salary. He would be there throughout my entire adolescence. Later—as soon as morning Sunday school was a thing of the past—I came to depend upon his weekly presence, rumbling admonitions and advice, raising his arms to invite prayer like some magnificent black eagle, exhorting his people to a love of mercy and kindness and justice and peace. I was deeply in love with Mr. Fraser, with goodness, and with God, and I had no idea which one was which.

My devotion to religion and to Mr. Fraser increased over the years. As soon as I could permanently trade Sunday school for church, I did. But long before that, I joined his church groups, did errands for him, served him. The Shirley Temple of that first Sunday changed into an eleven-year-old string bean, all elbows and knees and sparseness. But even I could recognize that my bright spirituality lent a poignant grace to my awkward form. Looking in the mirror, I gazed at this ungainly colt, and from my enormous eyes shone a light and a fervor that was more compelling than any lovely body. I would shut myself in the bathroom and recite psalms, repeat prayers, to those eyes in the mirror. Dreamlike, I would leave for school, for town, for trips, my mind turned inward to a life of sacrifice and devotion in the service of lepers, sinners, addicts, the world's afflicted and godless. I watched, my lip curled, as my peers embraced lipstick, giggles, dancing, the worship of noisy, pimply boys. I saw myself barefoot in foreign lands, handing out bread to the starving, whispering blessings, cradling diseased babies, leading whole multitudes in sacred song, flicking a hundred flies off my bare arms. And always, in these pictures, I could see Mr. Fraser at my side—forever handsome, unfailingly just and generous, profoundly desirable—praising me with his eyes and with his voice.

By the time I was fourteen, my spare body had filled out, and it was not hard to see that I had become one of those early bloomers who stun the onlooker with a fresh and surprising beauty. My huge eyes, my golden curls, my flawless skin, my *purity,* brought stares of admiration wherever I went. I gazed at myself and knew that it would take only wings to complete the picture.

By then, Mr. Fraser had received at least one honorary

doctorate of divinity, and I made a point of calling him Dr. Fraser at every opportunity. I led two Sunday school classes (now mercifully held in the afternoon), washed and ironed the church linens, held long conferences with Dr. Fraser about my future in the church. I tried to forget that he had a pretty wife—tall, black-haired, quick, and graceful—and four young children. It was unthinkable to me that they might be worthy of him. In my more vivid daydreams, I pictured him suffering under the tyranny of that dark witch of a woman, earnestly but with great forbearance, longing for freedom and for me. I kept away from the Manse, wanting all my contacts with him to be on holy ground.

One afternoon late in May, I returned to my home after a particularly long conference with Dr. Fraser. I had gone in to see him after school, and we had discussed, as usual, my future. We tossed my various options back and forth between us. Inner-city work, reaching out with healing hands to the urban homeless—infested with lice, crazed with drugs, staggering under the weight of alcohol and disease. Mentally I sidestepped the lice, and fixed my view on the cleaner aspects of addiction and sin. I pictured myself holding the grateful hands of young victims, as they lay in dark stairwells, thrashing in torment, their eyes wild with spiritual hunger. "Joanna! Joanna!" they would be crying. "Save me!" Behind me, standing in the shadows and imparting strength, would be Dr. Fraser, murmuring, "Yes, yes," and nodding his glad approval of my simple touch of mercy.

We had also discussed nursing, and I pictured myself bending low over my moaning patients, smoothing brows, quoting appropriate passages from the scriptures ("Blessed are they that mourn, for they shall be comforted"), listening for frail heartbeats. At moments of particular distress, I made the sign of the cross, and the patients smiled softly, instantly quiet and at peace. I was not troubled by these evidences of theological inconsistency. And no views of bedpans or vomit ever rose up to complicate the seductive medical scene.

We considered other avenues of service. African missions. Work with the hungry in Central America. Ministries with the Inuit in the frozen North, maybe in the barrens of Labrador. Teaching school to Native peoples. Programs to help the aged.

I was not drawn to teaching, and no bright pictures appeared to woo me. I did not care for children, and was irritated by their noisy carelessness, the selfish pursuit of their own desires. My mind skipped over and away from work with old people. Dimly, I saw a row of toothless men slumped in their chairs, hands blotched with brown marks, blue veins protruding. I juggled other possibilities in my head.

Dr. Fraser sat there in his mahogany desk chair, his elbows resting on the arms, his fingers pressed together to form a house or, more likely, a church. He smiled quietly, and his eyes were warm and accepting. "My dear Joanna," he said, and my heart lurched, as it always did, at the sound of his deep voice addressing me by name, "you are still very young. There is no need to rush into a decision. Your ultimate goal will unfold like a plant, like a verdant leaf, like your own emerging self, as you grow and mature. You may even find that you would like a pastoral job with some minister—like me, for instance—with whom you could work, visiting the sick, counseling the wicked, strengthening the weak. You do not have to go to the Congo, to Baffin Island, to find sin or suffering. And you can start your apprenticeship for that kind of work anytime you want to. This very week, in fact."

With one sentence, Dr. Fraser wiped off my screen of possible vocations the inner city, the medical profession, the Inuit, whole continents—Africa, South America, as well as the Arctic Circle. If I could serve God in this very room, it would be madness to look farther afield. Besides, there was an unscrutinized part of me that realized that Dr. Fraser might not, after all, be present in the wings of all those other stages I had so carefully set. Also, he was absolutely right. Here in the area of Sunnybrook Gardens, there was sin on all sides. Witness the hat hung with cherries on Good Friday; the lack of suitable piety before the start of every service—the whispering, the muffled chuckles; the shameful group who were agitating for a new minister; the unseemly fight within the congregation as to the design of the new stained glass window—should it be modern or traditional? Yes, indeed, there was sin to be dealt with in this very building.

"Yes! Oh, yes!" I cried. "How I would love to serve God in this very room. Or, of course, one like it."

Then I rose. It was almost suppertime, and I had to go. Blinded by the bright image of my future, I snatched up my books and file folders and prepared to leave.

He came out from behind his desk, and smiled his so benevolent smile at me. "God bless you," he said, as he always did, while I stood for a moment in the doorway. Usually he put his hand on my shoulder when he said it. This time, however, he put his hand on the back of my neck, and I could feel his index finger moving slowly up and down. "Good-bye, Joanna," he said, very softly.

He had touched me before. After all, I was used to that firm hand on my shoulder. Why was it, then, that I was suddenly visited by this hot bolt of joyful pain that traveled through my entire body like a sweet electric shock? Weak, I muttered, " 'Bye, Dr. Fraser," and floated down the corridor to the back door of the church hall.

I walked home through the late-afternoon fog, welcoming the strange blurred landscape, the vague forms, the sense of being adrift in a world in which all visible signposts had been altered. I felt disembodied; even the ground did not feel solid under my feet. Later, I ate my supper in silence, picking at my food, sighing a lot.

My mother counseled, "Eat your salad, dear. Your body needs the greens."

Greens! How could she speak of greens at such a time? "Oh, *Mother!*" I growled at her.

"Must be in love," chuckled my father. The look I delivered to him was pure hatred.

"Who is it, Joanna?" leered Robert. "Jonathan Hagan?" Jonathan Hagan was fifteen years old and our next-door neighbor. He had pink skin and orange hair and no coordination. Roger broke into fits of the giggles.

"Shut up!" I yelled, and flew from the table, knocking my chair over and spilling my milk.

Up in my room, I stood with my hand on my chest, eyes closed, trying to breathe normally. When I opened my eyes, I was looking at the pile of books I had brought home from school, via Dr. Fraser's office. A large brown envelope was sticking out from the bottom of the pile. I pulled it out. *"Urgent"* said a message on the top. It had been sent by Express Mail, but it was unopened. It was addressed to Dr. Gordon Fraser. Even in my state of hot confusion, I knew that this could not wait until tomorrow. I realized that I would have to walk up to the front door of that house I had never visited, and ring the doorbell. I didn't want to enter the home in which dwelled Dr. Fraser's witch. I was also very uneasy about walking outside at night. Fear of the dark was something that had plagued me since early childhood, except in the safety of my own house.

It was a warm May evening, and I wore no sweater over my red T-shirt and jeans. There were almost no streetlights in the neighborhood, and the fog was still thick. I was frightened as I walked along, startled by shadows, scarcely breathing, heart thumping.

When I reached the Manse, the veranda was in darkness; there was no outside light, and I climbed the steps carefully, lest I fall flat on my face. The front door was open, and I could see through the screen to the central hall. In front of

me were Dr. Fraser and the beautiful witch. He was dressed
in a checked shirt, and although still handsome, he did not
look one bit like an angel. He was frowning, and he spoke
to the witch in a harsh voice.

"Goddammit, Gloria! I can't help it if you *are* tired. I
worked like a slave all afternoon. Take the boys to the
hockey practice yourself. Motherhood is *your* territory, not
mine." His hands were flapping around in an inconclusive
way.

I stood welded to the veranda floor, afraid to move
forward or back, for fear I would be heard.

"Mommy!" A small face appeared around the corner of
the hall, tears streaming down its cheeks. The face be-
longed to a little girl, perhaps three years old—very small,
with a tangle of black hair like her mother's. She was
dressed in a pair of those heavy flannelette sleepers that zip
up the front—blue, and a little too big. A hand-me-down.
A straggle of hair was hanging in front of her left eye.
Child-hater though I was, some latent mother thing stirred
in me, and I longed to hold this child and to comfort her.
"I'm scared!" she cried, her voice high and uneven. "It's
dark. And I hear funny noises. Can I have the hall light on?
Please?"

"No!" snapped Dr. Fraser, without turning in her direction. "It's going to be dark every night of your life, so you'd better start getting used to it right now."

"But—" began the witch.

"Gloria!" stormed Dr. Fraser. "Don't undermine my authority. Are you trying to confuse the child as well as pamper her? You heard what I said. And so did she." He turned to face the forlorn figure, who was clutching her blanket, eyes wide and unblinking. "That's enough, Sonia," said Dr. Fraser. "Now get back to bed this minute."

Somewhere a baby started to cry. Dr. Fraser rubbed a limp hand across his brow. "For God's sake, Gloria," he said, "go do something with that baby! This place is a madhouse." He sat down on the hall stairs and put his face in his hands.

Two boys raced past their mother as she left the hall. "Hey, Dad!" one of them shouted. "We're ready! Let's go!"

"Sorry," moaned the figure on the stairs, "but I'm just too done-in to take you. If you had any idea of the backbreaking day I've just had, you wouldn't even ask me. Your mother'll do it."

"But we'll be late," protested the other boy. "Mom's in

there with the baby. The coach said he might kick us off
the team if we're ever late again."

Dr. Fraser looked slowly at each son, his eyes chilly. His
voice was cold, level. "You just decide, both of you, who
is more valuable, your coach or your father. Have you
heard all my sermons on unselfishness and not absorbed a
single word? Which is more important to you—your place
on the team or your father's weariness? I'm ashamed of
you. *Ashamed.*"

The witch appeared, her face stony—looking, in fact, a
great deal like a real witch. She was carrying the baby, who
was still crying. "We'll take her with us," she said to the
boys. "I'll put her in the car seat. I can nurse her in the
parking lot. Get a move on."

One of the boys grabbed her arm. "What's wrong,
Mom?" he asked, eyes troubled. "Are you mad? Did I do
something wrong?"

"No," she said. "I'm not mad at you. You did nothing
wrong. C'mon, or you'll be late."

I heard them go out the side door to the car, and prayed
that the car's headlights would fail to pick up my red
T-shirt. Sliding behind two bicycles beside the door, I
crouched down and made myself small. When the car

finally disappeared, I stood up again. The phone was ringing. It was sitting on a table beside the stairway, and Dr.
Fraser was able to pick it up without moving from his
perch on the step.

"Hello," he said. Then, "Oh, yes, Mrs. Halliday. Yes.
Yes, of course. No, you aren't disturbing me in the slightest. Oh, I'm so very sorry." The organ was playing again—
low, gentle; his gestures, even with no apparent audience
to see them, were firm again, relevant. "No, of course it's
not too late. Unfortunately, Gloria had to go out on a short
errand, and there's no one here to baby-sit. But when she
returns, I'll come right over. No. No, of course not. It's no
trouble at all. I'm not one whit tired, and it wouldn't
matter if I were. If you're worried, you'll need counsel.
And that's why God gave me this job. I'll see you about
nine thirty."

When he put down the receiver, I went to the bottom
of the veranda steps and then climbed them noisily.
Clumping across the floor, I reached the doorbell, and rang
it. The musical *bing-bong-bing* of the bell could not have
astonished me more if it had sung "Happy Birthday" in
Spanish.

When he saw me, Dr. Fraser offered his radiant smile.

"Joanna! My little missionary. What can have brought you here so late in the day?"

I tried not to look at his warm eyes, the slant of his cheekbones, the hair growing on the back of those large hands with their long and sensitive fingers.

He opened the screen door. "Come in, my dear," he said. "Come in. What a delight to see you."

I stood in the doorway and did not move. "I brought a letter," I said, scarcely audible. "It's Express Mail. It says 'Urgent' on the front. I took it home by mistake, with my books. I thought you should have it." I handed it to him.

"Generous and thoughtful, as always." He smiled at me, his face tender.

"Mommy! Mommy!" shrieked a voice from somewhere. "I'm so scared!"

I ran my tongue over my dry lips. "What's she scared of?" I asked.

"The dark, poor child." Dr. Fraser sighed, shaking his head. "Childhood is often a terrifying time."

I took a deep breath. Then I took another. Finally, I spoke. "When I was little, I was scared of the dark, too. My mother *and my father* let me keep the hall light on. It helped me. After a while, I didn't need it. Not in the house. I felt safe there. I still don't like the dark when I'm outside." I paused, courage growing. "You might try it," I said. "The hall light, I mean."

"Well!" he exclaimed. "What a good suggestion!" He called out to the stricken voice. "Just a minute, sweetheart. I'll be right there." Dr. Fraser looked at me. "Thank you," he said. "I'm getting used to your kind sensitivity. Won't you come in for a while?" He reached out, and once more those long fingers were on the back of my neck, and a flame shot through my chest.

"No, thank you," I said, sliding out from under his hand. "It's late." I looked at him from the other side of the closed screen door. "Very late." Then I paused. "And very dark," I added.

Then I turned around and, controlling the desire to run, I walked very carefully down the steps.

Much of the fog had cleared away by then, and on my way home, I looked at the bright windows of the houses. All the homes looked welcoming and warm. On all sides, the lit windows glowed golden in the dark night air, and I thought about the people on the other side of them. I also noticed that the leaves seen through the few streetlights were getting bigger, that soon they would be fully open and mature. Summer was not far off. Passing by Sally

Henderson's house, I remembered her large and friendly mother, with her wide smile and booming laugh. I thought about her jokes and about the peppermints that she carried around in her purse to hand out to all the kids, big and small. I wondered what Mrs. Henderson was like when her front door closed tight behind her laughter. A Coke can lay on the sidewalk, and I kicked it all the way home, hitting it so hard that it struck a tree and then went clanging over the curb and out onto the street. "There!" I cried, out loud.

At home, I opened the door and said to my mother as I entered the kitchen, "Sorry, Mom. I had to take a letter to Dr. Fraser. I found it among my books. I forgot to tell you I was going out."

She looked at me strangely. "Are you okay?" she asked. She came over and kissed me.

I touched her hair. "No," I said. "Not really okay. Not yet. But after a while I'll be all right. And at least . . ." I paused.

"At least what?" she asked.

"Oh, I dunno," I said. For a moment, my thought seemed to have gotten away from me. Then I remembered. "At least I know who you really are."

I climbed the stairs and went to bed. I lay awake for a

very long time, thinking about a lot of things, including the dark. Inside the house, the deep blackness felt very friendly. And I was surprised to realize that on my way home from Dr. Fraser's house—in spite of the absence of moon or stars—I had felt no fear. How could this be? I had no idea. Furthermore, under the weight of my sorrow, I could detect a strange lightness of spirit. None of this made sense to me. Never mind. I was tired and very sleepy. Maybe I'd think about all of it in the morning.

The Happy Pill

It is the year 2080. No nuclear bomb has been released upon the earth for many decades, but fear of it persists. Pollution is heavy and full of invisible threats: lungs, digestive systems, nervous responses, histamine levels are prey to its subtle ravages. However, there is still air out there to be breathed. In spite of international efforts and political fandances, the hole in the ozone layer still exists, but it is marginally smaller, and the greenhouse effect is temporarily stalled after a terrifying surge in the late 1990s. In some ways, therefore, life has not changed a great deal since the turn of the century.

The march of the biologists and chemists, however, has been onward and upward and very swift, bringing research teams nearer and nearer to cures for almost all the physiological ills that man has wreaked upon himself. Even environmental disorders are decreasing, as treatment of allergies becomes more and more sophisticated and effective. And there have been advances in other areas as well: the common cold has become uncommon; miscarriages—except for the intentional ones—are now out of the question; and couples can choose the sex, the size, the potential intellectual stature of their offspring before they are even conceived. More and more children are beautiful, highly intelligent, unmarked by deformities of any kind.

Of any kind? Well, perhaps not. Even the biochemists cannot claim so sweeping a victory as that. Deformity is an odd word, and difficult to define. It is true that skin is flawless: freckles and acne are found only in the fiction of earlier generations and in old photographs preserved by sentimental citizens. There are few diseases that cannot be cured by a needle or by a capsule; AIDS ceased to be a threat fifty years ago. Athletes run faster; singers reach higher notes; the color and texture of hair is a matter of choice (most whites choose blond and curly); most people die at the age of 125 or older, without arthritis, without wrinkles, without pain.

However, the nervous systems of humankind have been

harder to control. It is true that the jitters can be significantly stilled, but at the expense of alertness and of energy. Depression can be lifted, but with distressing side effects. Anger, fear, hatred, jealousy, grief, shyness, disappointment, frustration, resentment, cruelty—all these qualities have remained part of the human package.

Or so it seemed. But today, the amazing discovery of Dr. Peter Marzari, distinguished scientist from the Centre for Genetic Research at the University of Toronto, is a front-page item in the morning editions of all the major newspapers in North America.

Andrew Fitzpatrick has just reached out a fumbling hand to turn off the alarm. He frowns deeply. With all the technological advances of the last half century, surely someone could have invented a device capable of awakening a person without setting his entire nervous system on edge. A very alarming alarm indeed. Mind you, he knows that a clock radio could never do the job. It would take more than the trickle of a soft tune to tear away the thick skin of sleep, mercifully induced by last night's dose of Sleepalong. And he has found the newfangled Shockawake system even more upsetting than his alarm clock. Who wants to go to sleep knowing that some mysterious and remote-controlled shock wave is going to attack your left ear (or eye or testicle or throat—one is free to choose the anatomical location), right in the middle of a dream about Amelia Anstruther?

Amelia Anstruther is Andrew's secretary. She is very beautiful in an unorthodox way. That is to say, her nose is not straight, her mouth is overlarge, and her teeth are not arranged in the usual undeviating straight line. But she has clouds—yes, *clouds*—of wavy dark hair (no blond curls for Amelia), and her skin—on arms, on legs, and never mind thinking where else—is a daily assault on his fragile nerves, given its extreme softness and rosiness, its absolute inaccessibility.

But even without her skin and her masses of dark hair, Amelia would be essential to Andrew. Andrew is thirty-nine years old, and a successful and prosperous writer. His novels are, as they say, "widely acclaimed," and quite rightly so. He is spilling over with sensitivity and imagination and brains. (His mother saw to *that,* having taken two capsules of Everbrain the very night he was conceived.) But Andrew is uncoordinated and mechanically inept, and has to do his writing with a pen instead of a machine. He often grieves that the two pills that now regulate coordination and mechanical aptitude were invented just six months after he was born. But then, he thinks, as he stares at the bedroom ceiling, if I had been able to cope with either a typewriter or a word processor, I never would have met Amelia. And although Amelia—being both married and unattracted to him—is unavailable to him in his real life, she is a willing collaborator in both his sleeping and his waking dreams.

Andrew, thinking of Amelia's distance from him, is already depressed. He is also tired; he stopped writing at 1:30 last night. He would like to lie in bed all day, reading the kinds of books he would be ashamed to write. He hopes that his wife, long out of bed and downstairs, feeding and steering and advising their blond and curly-headed son and daughter, won't bring him a cup of coffee. Or worse still, a breakfast tray. He doesn't want to feel either grateful or guilty. He doesn't want to see her patient, kindly face, or her sparse and uncombed hair, until he feels a little stronger. Simply by being alive and in the same room with him, she awakens harsh thoughts within his breast. Her sweetness assaults him like an insult, knowing, as he does, that he is not patient, is not kindly. Her uncombed hair infuriates him, and always he sees behind that frizzy and tangled mop a vision of Amelia, hovering ghostlike against the white wall, on the empty TV screen, or behind the door, her hair tumbling richly over her soft, white shoulders.

Andrew has still not budged—except to thrash and fidget. He has made no attempt to rise. He lies there and thinks about his own sins—mostly internal ones; after all, he has never stolen anything, or assaulted or murdered or intentionally cheated anyone. But he does do a lot of full-bodied hating, and his chest (Andrew always feels that negative emotions emanate from the chest, rather than from the head or from some filmy disembodied soul) is full of finely tuned resentments and outrage. He is furious at governments for starting wars or failing to legislate wisely, and for continuing to permit pollution to sully the air he breathes. He is irritated at the poor for not pulling up their economic socks. When his writing moves slowly and without real flair, he is wild with frustration, with unmasked anger: at his pen, which scratches; at the noise of the dishwasher downstairs; at his daughter, for taking overlong in the bathroom; at his son, for having a placid and happy nature; at the weather, for being foggy; at his mother, for having permitted his adolescent immaturities; at his wife, for suffering his transgressions in silence. He abhors servility in women, but knows (with genuine self-loathing) that he couldn't survive two weeks if Dora didn't make his meals and brew his coffee and wash his socks, and do all those things that women were supposed to have stopped doing almost a century ago.

Andrew closes his eyes. How can anyone as flawed as he is write such wonderful books? But consider Wagner. He was a lot more sinful than Andrew, and look at the magnificent music he was able to produce. It seems to Andrew that the gods are often operating in a state of confusion. He burrows more deeply into his pillow and lets his mind wallow in a dense contemplation of war, disease, injustice, grief, and hunger. "Dammit," he mumbles, "where's that woman with my coffee?"

As if on cue, Dora appears, kicking open the door (confound her—she'll have that paint scraped right off within a month), poking her frizzy head into the room. She is carrying a tray. On the tray are three fig bars (his favorite), a mug of strong, black, sugared coffee, a hot-cross bun, a hard-boiled egg, and one rose. The rose rebukes him. He adds regret and shame to the other miseries that assail him. But his mind is already deep into a short story, the principal plot and character having emanated from his morning's contemplation of cosmic sin. His novel will now be at war with his short story, and heaven only knows which will win. He wants to write them simultaneously, but he knows that for him this is impossible. He doesn't thank Dora, not even for the rose. He dives at his coffee savagely. A miner, trapped underground for nine days, will attack soup in much the same way when it is offered to him at the exit.

"Your paper," says Dora, and leaves him. Not "my paper" or even "our paper." He winces, the more so because he knows she hasn't meant to abuse him.

When he unfolds the newspaper, the headline, huge and block-lettered, leaps out from the page and demands his full attention. MIRACLE PILL PROMISES HAPPINESS. He reads on, gobbling up two of his fig bars without tasting them, forgetting to finish his coffee.

Apparently the pill is perfect. Tested for safety, side effects, efficacy, birth defects, speed of action, it seems to have met and passed every trial. Andrew reads that it lifts the spirits without causing drowsiness or dullness of wit, or even any form of unbridled or vulgar euphoria; you can still drive a car; you may still, thank heavens, drink. Safe for pregnant women, diabetics, the weak, and the aged, it will eliminate anxiety, quiet fears, smother hate, stamp out aggression, squelch guilt, and foster joy. "What's more," says the quotation from Dr. Peter Marzari, "it acts quickly, and will register a significant mood change—not to say philosophical turnaround—within one hour." Taken in the right dosages and over a long enough period of time, it will also bring about salutary mutations in genetic structures. One may expect, therefore, that the children of the users of this pill will be lighthearted and peaceful people. "Think," says Dr. Marzari, "what this will mean for the human race."

What, indeed? As Andrew reads the last sentence in the article, he is already out of bed and pulling on his socks: "As a result of long-term and exhaustive testing, this pill will be available immediately in pharmacies throughout the country, starting today. Because of its proven safety, no prescriptions will be necessary."

Andrew leaves the tray on the bed, with its one remaining half-gnawed fig bar, its mug of tepid coffee. Later on, the cat will knock over the cup and spill coffee through three layers of covers. Dora will feel angry about this as she completely changes the bed (freshly made up yesterday); but true to form, she will mention this fact to no one.

On the way out of the house, Andrew chastises his children for dawdling over their breakfasts.

"But it's Saturday, Dad," they whine, in unison.

"I don't care if it's New Year's Day," he snarls. "You're young. You should be up and doing. I worked halfway through the night, and look at *me*. *I'm* up and out." He knows this is unpleasant and unjust, but he also knows that once he has one of those pills in his system—and another and another, as day follows day—he will be sweet and kindly, forever and ever. So he takes a certain ghoulish pleasure in this swansong of domestic meanness.

"Is it necessary to wear that ridiculous pink T-shirt *every day*?" he growls at his son. "I thought pink was for girls." And to his beautiful blond daughter, who is setting out a game of solitaire to the left of her bowl of Evergrain, he snaps, "Cards! With the kind of planned intelligence we arranged for you—and *paid* for—I can't see why your report card isn't composed entirely of A's. A good brain is useless if you're born lazy. Discipline yourself. Look at *me*! I make myself work even when I could be bicycling in the park or watching TV."

Andrew tries not to think about what he has just said. He loathes bicycling and he hates TV. It is no virtue on his part that he writes every day of his life. It's the only thing he really likes to do. His writing is his lifeline, his way of coping with the negative forces that continually assail him, his retreat from despair. Bring order out of chaos, he often says, and it is no longer chaos. Who would choose to go to the park—particularly on a bicycle—or watch TV, if they could do such a saving, such a heroic thing as *write?*

As Dora appears in the doorway, he says, "For God's sake, Dora, can't you at least comb that hair of yours?"

Halfway to the drugstore, he sees Amelia, out doing her marketing with her handsome husband. "Hi, beautiful," he mutters under his breath, and his whole body is knotted with longing for her.

Although it is only 9:30 when he reaches Main Street, he has to line up outside the pharmacy for almost thirty minutes in order to get his pills.

Lucky it isn't raining, he muses. Not that they'd care. Stupid damn store for not hiring more staff on the day a hot item is featured. Confounded woman ahead keeps backing up and stepping on my foot. Bet they run out of pills before I get to the head of the line. They must think I've got nothing better to do with my time than wait on this godforsaken sidewalk—spending half the morning with a bunch of losers, when I'm at such a crucial point in my novel.

Andrew's face softens for the first time since awakening that morning. His novel! The true love of his life is not, after all, Amelia Anstruther, but his work. He thinks of the way a story grows out of his fingers—yes, his *fingers*—as his mind scuttles around and behind them, trying to make

159

them move faster. The chapter he plans to work on today (the second-to-last chapter) is the one most central to the whole book. He feels like a mountain climber on the verge of attacking the highest peak. The challenge exhilarates him in a way that few people could share or understand. He looks around at the disgruntled faces in the line (all of them unhappy people, or they wouldn't be there), and pities every one of them who is not a writer. He feels such a sudden surge of joy that for a moment he wants to embrace the cross woman beside him who is audibly muttering curses under her breath and chewing bubble gum with her mouth open.

Andrew sighs, and shifts from one foot to the other. His brief moment of delight has passed, and he returns to thoughts of mortgage payments, squabbles with his editor over the use of semicolons, late royalty payments, the plight of the whales and the caribou and the almost extinct rain forests, the men who may eventually rape his ten-year-old daughter, the evil youths who will someday lead his son in the direction of liquor and drugs and unbridled sex, the shameful way he treats his generous and uncomplaining wife, the unseemly and futile lust that he feels for Amelia, the inadequate equipment of the town's fire department, the unfortunate results of the last federal election, cockroaches, bats, procrastination, death. By the time Andrew reaches the head of the line, he almost snatches the bottle away from the pharmacist.

He does not go home, however. It is a twenty-minute walk, and he has lost too much time already. Within one hour, the newspaper article said, the pill would be doing its job. He goes into a restaurant, orders a cup of coffee, and swallows one of the pills. The brand name is Paradico. He curls his lip at such lack of subtlety, and spends the next fifteen minutes inventing names and writing them on his paper napkin. They are all as trite as Paradico, and this depresses him enormously.

Andrew decides he will not return home until the pill has had time to work completely. He wants to greet his family with his new personality intact. Maybe he will shock Dora by bringing her flowers. And perhaps a small gift for each child. In an hour's time, he may feel like buying them. Without mirth, he chuckles to think of how surprised his family will be. He resolves not to reveal to them the source of his new nature, whatever form it may take. Let them think it is the result of some sudden spiritual explosion.

When the waitress finally appears, he orders bacon and eggs, explaining to her sternly that the eggs must be turned over and the yolks firm. He is irritated to discover that the toast appears before his bacon and eggs, and he kicks the side of the table leg to register his impatience at the delay. However, the rest of his meal eventually appears—on a visibly greasy plate, accompanied by a wilted sprig of parsley. Although the eggs are runny, he quite enjoys them, mopping up what remains of the yolk with his cold toast. He looks at the names written on his napkin, and thinks that they are perhaps not as stupid as he had thought. Even Paradico is a rather clever invention.

He then leaves the restaurant and meanders about the town in search of gifts. He picks out a pink baseball hat for his son (he does, after all, seem to like the color), and a card game for his daughter (who should be having a little fun—she'll only be young once). He orders a dozen white carnations for Dora, but then suddenly remembers that she loves yellow—something he hasn't thought of in perhaps ten years.

Armed with a large bouquet of yellow roses and daisies, he leaves the store, whistling. Upon reaching the street, he catches a glimpse of Amelia Anstruther and her husband, walking hand in hand, gazing into each other's eyes. Andrew smiles tenderly, admiring their youth and their love for one another.

On the way home, Andrew doesn't hurry. He walks

slowly, tasting the bright morning sunshine, the fresh spring air, observing the blossoming trees, the greening grass, a flight of geese on their way north. His house, when it comes into view, looks very satisfying to him. His eyes slide over the broken veranda and settle on the building's balanced lines. Given the dimensions of the front of the structure, he can see that the proportions of the roof and its pitch are exactly right. And best of all, his family is inside.

Andrew reaches down and strokes the cat before entering the house, and she breaks into a loud, surprised purr. From the doorway, he can see that Dora is working on the family finances. As he enters, she looks up from the bills without enthusiasm. "Hi, Andrew," she says. He looks at her and sees her tired eyes, her small, straight nose, the long, graceful fingers that are holding the *Income Tax Guide*. He does not notice her hair. "For you," he announces, holding out the flowers. "And for you, and you!" he cries, as the children emerge from the TV room. He has to control his desire to sing, to dance, so strong is his feeling of love for these excellent people.

His family is, of course, dumbfounded. But everything that happens delights him: the longish silence that follows his announcement of gift-giving, the quite insulting look of shock on their faces, and then their extravagant joy in

163

the gifts. He sits there, smiling, smiling, savoring their thanks, their hugs, their kisses. Inside his pocket, he rubs the bottle of Paradico pills between his thumb and his forefinger, making love to the source of all this joy.

"Now," he says cheerfully, when the rituals of gratitude have gone on long enough, "I must get to work. My novel is calling me, and I'm itching to get at it. I've been looking forward to writing this particular chapter all month. See you all at supper."

Andrew climbs the stairs to the third floor of his house, to the room where he does his writing. It is small, sparsely furnished, cluttered with papers and file folders and chewed pencils. It looks as inviting to him as a palace, a harem, a garden full of tropical birds. And so it has always been for him. He enters, sits down, and, as is his custom, rereads the last chapter he has written. It seems altogether wonderful. The writing, he feels, is balanced and skillful. The plot is suspenseful and intricately devised. His handling of conflict, of pain, of human suffering is superb. There is nothing, not one word or comma, that he would want to change. This seems odd to him, because this is his first draft; the words came straight out of his pen onto the paper, as fast as he could write them down. However, he wastes no time fretting about this strange state of affairs.

Instead, he takes his pen out of the empty beer can on his desk and looks at the blank page.

The chapter that awaits him is Chapter 16, out of a total of seventeen chapters. It is the key chapter. After it is written, the final chapter will simply draw the remaining threads together into a satisfying resolution of the central conflicts. He has known all along that there will be no Hollywood finish, that there will be an open kind of ending to the work. Nonetheless, he has planned a culmination, a satisfying artistic treatment of all the painful, interlocking components of the story. But it is in Chapter 16 that he will deal with the novel's real climax. In this chapter he will bring into focus all the basic themes: the hero's unrequited love, his struggle with a growing cancer, his sense of failure and lack of fulfillment, his concern for the planet's sickness and impending death, and what Andrew has referred to as his "cosmic scream of pain"—a phrase which he now thinks he may have unintentionally lifted from somewhere. But, no matter.

Andrew sits in front of the blank page for one hour. He is in a real quandary, but the problem fails to worry him. Unrequited love, cancer, failure, the earth's illness—what are these to him? Nothing. He simply does not care. He cannot describe that "cosmic scream of pain" because he can no longer hear it. The endeavor is clearly a pointless one. Of course, he can solve many of the difficulties by fixing everything. Let his hero win his love in the last chapter, let his cancer be cured, let him succeed in some large enterprise so that his sense of failure will dissolve, let the world's governments clear up the pollution and ban the bomb, let the scream of pain be converted into a resonant hymn of thanksgiving.

Yes, he can certainly do all of those things. But what about Chapter 16? Without Chapter 16, the novel contains one large and gaping hole. But Andrew does not feel up to dealing with pain and suffering today. Once again he caresses his bottle of pills, and chuckles quietly. Once those pills are widely used—and they will certainly be almost universally taken—no one will ever want to read a book like this one. A generation from now, he realizes, they won't even know what I'm talking about. Long before then, my novel will be a museum piece, a curiosity. To finish this work would be a ridiculous waste of useful energy, close though it is to completion. In fact, he muses, as he lays down his pen, to write *any* other novel—or short story, for that matter—would be equally futile. All novels have conflicts, problems, at the roots of their plots. They contain characters who are tormented by life. People and

circumstances wrestle with one another on a stage that is
slippery with tears. And such things, Andrew realizes, are
not only irrelevant, they are also of no interest to him. Not
anymore. Nor can he, for the life of him, understand why
he ever felt differently.

It does seem something of a pity to Andrew to lose the
pleasure he has always derived from writing, but perhaps he
can turn to a form more in keeping with his new self. Lyric
poetry may be just the thing. He can spend his working
hours in a musical outpouring of praise, of love—celebrat-
ing the perfection of birds, sunsets, trees, flowers, youth,
small furry animals—although he does wonder why one
need write about such things. Why not simply relax and
enjoy them? Besides, he has never written poetry, nor has
he ever had the least urge to do so. However, given time,
undoubtedly a convenient muse will emerge, providing
the appropriate poetic motivation.

Mind you, there may not be much potential income in
all of this, but that doesn't worry Andrew in the slightest.
Everything will work out just splendidly. He is absolutely
sure of this. For one thing, he won't need Amelia's secre-
tarial skills anymore—lyric poems tending to be short and
easily transcribed—and this will be a significant financial
saving. His publishers may be a bit frazzled by this turn of

events, but he is certain that he'll be able to explain his point of view to them, to their complete satisfaction.

Andrew stuffs his manuscript away in the bottom drawer of his desk, and decides to go down to share his decision with his family. Humming a little tune under his breath, he descends the two staircases very slowly, eager to hear their reactions, but savoring the suspense. He has always saved the frosting on his cakes until the last possible moment. He carries his bottle of pills with him in his pants pocket. He doesn't want to be separated from them for even five minutes.